THE SECRETS OF SAM & SAM

www.**randomhousechildrens**.co.uk

Also by Susie Day

Pea's Book of Best Friends
Pea's Book of Big Dreams
Pea's Book of Birthdays
Pea's Book of Holidays

You can find Susie at
www.susieday.com *or* @mssusieday
facebook/Susie Day-Writer

SUSIE DAY

THE SECRETS OF SAM & SAM

Illustrated by Aaron Blecha

RED FOX

THE SECRETS OF SAM AND SAM
A RED FOX BOOK 978 1 782 95261 9

First published in Great Britain by Red Fox Books,
an imprint of Random House Children's Publishers UK
A Penguin Random House Company

Penguin
Random House
UK

This edition published 2015

1 3 5 7 9 10 8 6 4 2

Penguin Random House is committed to a sustainable future for
our business, our readers and our planet. This book is made
from Forest Stewardship Council® certified paper.

MIX
Paper from
responsible sources
FSC® C018179

Set in 13/18pt Baskerville MT by Falcon Oast Graphic Art

Red Fox Books are published by Random House Children's Publishers UK,
61–63 Uxbridge Road, London W5 5SA

www.randomhousechildrens.co.uk
www.totallyrandombooks.co.uk
www.randomhouse.co.uk

Addresses for companies within The Random House Group Limited can be found
at: www.randomhouse.co.uk/offices.htm

THE RANDOM HOUSE GROUP Limited Reg. No. 954009

A CIP catalogue record for this book is available from the British Library.

Printed and bound in Great Britain by
CPI Group (UK) Ltd, Croydon CR0 4YY

for Lynda

Hollalleog, Suilven, Griphook!

1

SECRET #1:

SAM PAGET-SKIDELSKY IS A SUPERHERO

'I'm ready. I'm ready now. Can we go? Are we leaving?'

Sam pulled on his spider-web socks and his spider web hat, and hurried downstairs to the kitchen.

'Yes, Sam, this is exactly the outfit I've chosen to wear out of the house,' said Mum K dryly, pointing to the soggy towel wrapped around her head.

'Haircuts, *then* cinema,' said Mum Gen, steering Sam towards a kitchen chair beside his sister.

'No!' she yelled, folding her arms and hunching up her shoulders. 'It's *my* hair on *my* head and you can't make me chop it off! My hair has *human rights*.'

'I'm not at all sure it does,' said Mum Gen, flexing the scissors doubtfully.

Sam tugged a bit of his fringe, where it flopped into his eyes. 'Hmm. It *is* alive.'

'See?'

Mum K scratched at her towel. 'Your argument would be more persuasive if you hadn't quite cheerfully dyed the dog green last week, Sam.'

Surprise dribbled on his fuzzy blanket-bed by way of protest. (He'd been washed six times, but still looked vaguely mouldy.)

'I'm not Sam, I'm Sammie!' Sammie shouted, scrunching down even further in her chair.

The Paget-Skidelskys were two mums, two Sams and a puppy – or they had been until four weeks ago. Sammie had been Sam too – or Sam Two – for eleven years, until she loudly declared herself Samara, then Samanda, briefly Jennifer-Jo, and finally Sammie, in a permanent, written-on-the-register way. Mum Gen said it was a natural evolution, like a tadpole to a frog.

Sam wasn't going to bother with it. Everyone already liked him just the way he was.

'That's dog hair. Dog hair doesn't have human rights,' Sammie continued, ducking away as Mum Gen attempted to sneak up on her with a comb.

'Aha – but should it?' Mum K leaned in close. 'Does it have dogs' rights? Is it a human right to have more rights than a dog?'

Mum Gen groaned. 'I can't do philosophy *and* haircuts on a Sunday morning. Please, pick one, or we will never get out of the house.'

Soon, Sam's once-living floppy hair was in tragic dead bits all over the kitchen floor.

Sammie, however, wouldn't let the scissors near.

'But you've always had the same haircut,' said Mum Gen, frowning as she looked from twin to twin.

This was true. The Sams were not identical – boy-girl twins never are – but that hadn't ever stopped people from mixing them up. There were photographs dotted all around the house: two matching figures in stripy tops and jeans, with narrow freckly faces and floppy brown hair that turned curly at the tips of the ears.

HOW TO TELL SAMS APART

extra freckles and heroic ears

smells of pencils

SAM

wider face

scar under chin from riding bike up tree

smells of burning/ explosions/ permed dog

SAMMIE

But now Sammie's hair was swept across her forehead into a clip with a banana on it, the rest long enough to tuck behind her ears and tickle her collar – while Sam's was, by the looks of it, mostly on the kitchen floor.

Mum K joined Mum Gen to stare.

'Appalling,' she said, resting her soggy-towelled head on Mum Gen's shoulder. 'When did our babies turn into such decrepit grown-ups, eh?'

'We're *eleven*, you weirdo,' said Sammie. 'You want to get new glasses.'

Mum Gen raised an eyebrow pointedly.

Sammie rolled her eyes. 'Mum K, I'm sorry for calling you a weirdo,' she said, in a dreary sing-song voice. 'This was wrong because I'm not meant to say things like that, even if they are undeniably true because of . . . reasons. In future, I will only call you a weirdo when you aren't here.'

This was known as Sampologizing, and usually resulted in long dull arguments that Sam didn't listen to – but apparently Mum Gen was too distracted now to bother.

'You don't mind not having the same hair, Sam?' asked Mum Gen in her Professionally Gentle voice, resting one hand on his shoulder. 'I think it might be a twin's right to mind.'

When she wasn't being their mum/hairdresser, Mum Gen was Dr Paget: Child Psychologist and Family Therapist. She listened to unhappy people on velvety golden sofas in their front room, deploying the Professionally Gentle voice until they stopped being unhappy. Every now and then she forgot to turn it off.

MUM GEN

nice face

cardigan

soothing tea

MUM K

Scary big brain

sarcastic eyebrow of doom

black coffee

POW!

Sam liked the Professionally Gentle voice. He felt like a rabbit having its ears stroked.

'I don't care about hair,' he said, 'so long as no one tries to put any bananas in mine.'

Sam cared about *Spider-Man 5*, which was starting in twenty-eight minutes. And they had to leave time for buying popcorn.

'Fine!' said Mum Gen, dropping the scissors in defeat. 'Your hair has rights, Sammie. At least it does this morning.'

'Ha!' Sammie hopped off the chair with a smirk, and prodded Mum K's elbow. 'I'm just being helpful, giving you more fascinating things about me to put in your book.'

'You're all heart.'

When she wasn't being their other mum, Dr Skidelsky was also a Child Psychologist and Family Therapist – but the sort without a golden sofa. She mostly wore superhero T-shirts and jeans, but underneath she was terribly serious and clever. Ever since the Sams were small, she'd spent weekdays in Edinburgh, teaching at the university and researching her book: an important-sounding one about having two children named Sam. ('Sammie' was a rather unwelcome development; it meant adding a whole new chapter.) Every Sunday evening they used to wave her off as she headed for King's Cross station and the sleeper train, and not see her again until Friday.

But not any more. Now that she was ready to write the book, she was going to stay in London all week too. Tomorrow they would begin the New Routine, and be two mums, two Sams and a puppy all the time.

Sam liked that too. One mum was good. Two mums was best.

Ten minutes later they were striding through the park towards the Lexi Cinema, Mum K now with bright blue streaks in her hair like a mad badger.

Sundays were Paget-Skidelsky Family Days Out. After Mum Gen got home from church, they would head off together for important bonding and arguments, within a strict monthly budget. On Sam's turn to pick, it was always the Science Museum or the cinema. The Science Museum had rockets and actual real astronaut gloves, and upstairs you could try on actual real spacesuits and have your picture taken (Sam had three already) – and once they'd stayed in the shop so long the security guards had begun to shut the doors and they were almost locked in all night, to sleep under the big white rocket and the endless bouncing light of the huge energy wheel . . .

But new *Spider-Man* was even better.

Spidey spun and bounced and heroically saved multiple humans, a herd of cows and a pretty girl. (His mums grumbled at that bit – 'She could have done that herself!') He swung off high buildings without a care. He was basically Samazing.

Sam watched it all intently, pencil in hand, for tips.

He was Co-Creator and Head Illustrator of *The Continuing Adventures of Captain Samazing* – his own invented comic for only certain people to see. Captain Samazing looked a tiny bit like Buzz Lightyear, but mostly like Sam. Only wider. And made of pencil. And in space. Captain Samazing didn't have superpowers, but he had a spaceship (the *Pocket Rocket*) and a sidekick called Pointy to help his endless battle with intergalactic squids, and one day someone was going to make films based on his comics too, definitely.

That night, after dinner, instead of Mum K hauling her wheelie suitcase down the road and vanishing for another week as usual, she joined Sam and Mum Gen in their traditional Sunday night spot, to watch *Tiny Robot Unicorn Friends*.

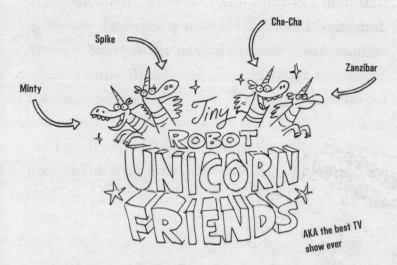

There were only two squashy bean-bag chairs tucked into the kitchen corner by the little TV, so Sam sat on a cushion, resting against Mum Gen's knees. Sammie eyed the scene suspiciously, then squeezed in too in front of Mum K.

'What *is* this?' said Mum K, wrinkling her nose as the first unicorn powered across the screen on pneumatic hooves.

'Only the best TV show in the universe, Kara,' said Mum Gen. 'Now shush. No talking during Unicorn Hour.'

Mum K ignored her entirely, and kept loudly whispering, 'Who's she?' and 'How did they get over there?' and 'Oh, that's clever, that's an *homage* to *Battleship Potemkin*, did you know that?' – until Mum Gen put a hand over her mouth. After that she stayed quiet, apart from the occasional stifled chuckle.

That night Sam went to sleep wearing his spider-web socks, the *Tiny Robot Unicorn Friends* theme song playing in his head.

We're robots and we're tiny,
We're never ever whiny,
Our metal's super-shiny
AND WE WANNA BE YOUR FRIENDS!

CAPTAIN'S LOG: SUNDAY

SPIDER-MAN 5: ACHIEVED.

EPISODES OF TINY ROBOT UNICORN FRIENDS
WATCHED: 1

SQUIDS DRAWN: 17

CONCLUSIONS: BEST DAY EVER,
A++++. WOULD RELIVE AGAIN IF
TRAPPED IN TIME VORTEX

2

Dear Mum K,

I think your book should be called SAMMIE'S BOOK
and be all about me.

   Not twins.

   Just me.

   This is why:

1) There are too many books about twins already. You
have about ten.

2) A book about one person is always better than a
book about two people. Like it isn't 'Harry Potter and
Janet and the Philosopher's Stone'. Janet is just going to
get in the way. KILL STUPID JANET.

3) I'm not being mean or anything but we all know I am
the Best Twin. A book about Sam would just be him in a
chair going 'Lala spaceships' and eating sandwiches and

smiling while magical sparkles fart out of his bottom.
With me you have DRAMA and EXCITEMENT and
DANGER.

4) I know your book is a boring one only boring people
like you will ever read, but if you add loads of cool stuff
about me being amazing, then it could be like a shock
crossover hit and there could be a film and I could be in
the film. On skis. Fighting bears. With javelins. (Films of
books always add stuff that's not in the book, it's OK.)
Then we will be rich and you can buy me a car/some
javelins.

5) You have to put the dog in it though.

SAMMIE'S BOOK (with special guest star Surprise the
Dog). Call it that.

   Write back NOW and say YES or it means you
don't love me.

From Sammie

Sammie whittled the end of her javelin into the
sharpest point the bread knife could manage, arched
her back and let fly.

13

The javelin (it was the white plastic pole of a patio umbrella really, with the flowery shade snapped off) sailed high into the Monday morning blue sky, over the rusty monkey bars at the bottom of the garden, over the target swinging on the door of the shed, and over the back wall. She watched it drop out of sight. Far in the distance came the happy tinkle of breaking glass.

Sammie grinned, and reached for another stick.

It wasn't her fault she'd missed. She'd asked for a proper javelin for her birthday last week, and a proper javelin would've hit that swinging target square in the face. (The target was a squashy old pillow with a girl drawn on it: blue-eyed and swishy-haired, with pale pink spectacles and two big dots for nostrils; the sort of face that deserved a good javelin-ing.) She'd asked for a proper penknife too, because it was hard to whittle the end off a not-javelin (this one was a broom handle) with a bread knife without stabbing yourself in the leg a bit. But no, it was all school supplies and book tokens and, mortifyingly, from Granny Freya, a bra.

White cotton, stretchy, with red strawberries on.

The only consolation was that Granny Freya

always gave the Sams matching presents – *Twins ought to look like twins, don't you think?* – and Sammie had the pleasure of watching Sam nervously pick up his own squashy parcel and reluctantly peel back the sticky tape to unwrap it.

But his had been socks.

Emily Roche didn't have a bra. Emily Roche, with her swishy hair and her pale pink spectacles and her stealing-Sammie's-chair-next-to-Reema-at-school. Emily was like a doll: neat, dainty; her head would come off with a satisfying pop if you pulled her hair hard enough, probably.

Confusingly, Sammie felt fairly certain that, while having a bra for your birthday was criminally grim, not having a bra ought to be worse, because bras were old and old was best. (She was nine minutes older than Sam, which was why she was so totally definitely the Best Twin.) So when Emily Roche had watched her changing for PE, and saw her stretchy cotton strawberry print, and whispered to Reema behind her little doll's hand – whispered and giggled as if Sammie was doing something wrong, as if Sammie was breaking some secret Class Six rule that no one had mentioned – well, that wasn't fair at all.

Sammie weighed the broom handle in her palm, finding the balance, then drew her arm back and hurled it as hard as she could.

Plop, went the javelin, arcing high then driving hard into the middle of the lawn. It quivered, then toppled over, uprooting a big chunk of grass.

Sammie glared at the innocent, unstabbed face on the pillow. Maybe she should've asked for a bow and arrows for her birthday. Anyone would want to be best friends with a girl who had a bow and arrows.

Thwump!

The sound came from inside the house, high up.

Sammie shaded her eyes against the morning sun and peered up. Through the little window on the landing she saw a sudden white blur, and there was another loud *thwump!* – this time followed by a high-pitched whine of pain.

Surprise.

Sammie sprinted through the back door and hurtled up the stairs – to find two dusty cardboard boxes on the landing, one of which had split open on hitting the carpet and spewed forth piles of typed white paper. Beside it, her brother was already clutching a whimpering, wriggling Surprise tightly in his arms.

'He's all right,' Sam promised, catching her eye. 'Just a bit spooked.'

'Did nasty Mum K drop a box on your head?' crooned Sammie, giving Surprise's green-tinged ears a comforting ruffle.

Surprise dribbled mournfully all over her wrist. (He was still a puppy really; a teething one who left trails of dribble, chewed things and the occasional tooth in his wake – which made a nice change from puddles of wee, according to Mum Gen, and didn't, according to Mum K.)

'I told the ridiculous animal to get out of the way!' came Mum K's voice, crossly floating down from the attic above.

A folding metal ladder led up to an open trap-door set into the ceiling.

Mum Gen stepped out of their bedroom, pinning her wispy brown hair up into a sort of knot and staring unhappily at the mess. 'Do you have to start hurling boxes around *now*?' she called up. 'You have remembered you're taking the twins to school?

And usually I feed them before that happens. Sammie – is that blood on your leg?!'

'Only a bit. What are you doing?' Sammie clanked steadily up the ladder, and swung her slightly stabbed leg over the lip of the trapdoor and into the attic.

It was a gloomy room, with one small slanted window set into the slope of the roof at the front, and a single bare light bulb hanging from the ceiling. Stacked high in every corner was the usual grimy clutter: old lampshades, suitcases, a tartan picnic blanket; multiple cardboard boxes, labelled *SAMS: 18–24 MONTHS* and *LANG. DEV'MENT: NOTES*; and, covered in cobwebs, some actually important stuff.

'Lego pirate ship!' Sammie recognized the twisty palm tree at once, and dragged the box out under the light bulb to root through all the bits of boat and tiny plastic swords. Sam had wanted space Lego that year, but she'd sat on him until he wrote a new letter to Father Christmas, declaring his sudden change of allegiance. She slotted a cannonball into the cannon, and leaned over the edge, aiming carefully.

The cannonball pinged off Sam's head.

'Ow,' he said.

'Come up! There's tons of our old stuff up here!'

Sam slipped Surprise off his lap and gripped the ladder. He put one foot on the first rung, and tentatively climbed up to rung number four.

Then he shut his eyes and climbed straight back down, and in a rather pale voice said he would much prefer to stay right where he was and look after the dog, just in case, thank you very much.

Sammie sighed. *See? No one would ever want to read a book about* that *Sam.*

Under the pirate ship was more ancient treasure: a telephone on wheels, some rubbishy drawings Sam had done (aged five, according to his wonky handwriting), and a grubby plastic rabbit whose ears moved up and down and made a carrot go in and out of its mouth. It made a horrible grinding noise and played a plinky tune as it did so. Sammie didn't remember it at all, and threw it down with all Mum K's rubbish.

Mum Gen picked it up with a misty smile. 'Whirry Bunny,' she sighed. 'This used to be in your cot when you were tiny—'

'Oi, stop that! We're not keeping it!' shouted Mum K.

'But—'

'No! First it'll be Whirry Bunny, next it'll be Frankie Blankie—'

'Oh, *Frankie Blankie*,' said Mum Gen, in a dreamy voice.

Mum K stamped her foot. 'No! This is a clear-out. That means throwing things away, not cooing at them and then putting them back!'

'But,' said Sammie, grabbing the pirate ship and clutching it to her chest, 'not the pirate ship. And look – that's my shell collection. And the doll's house that Big Uncle Boris made. You can't chuck them out. That's like our whole actual childhood.'

Mum Gen put her hands on her hips. 'See? I'm trying to protect our children's beloved possessions!'

Mum K glared. 'No you're not, you're being a weird hoarder who can't bear to throw anything away – which is why this attic is so full of junk.'

'It's not junk!' said Sammie. 'We might change our minds and want to play with it again.'

You were allowed to still like Lego, even when people gave you a bra for your birthday.

'You didn't even know it was up here!'

'It's not only *their* things, Kara dear,' said Mum

20

Gen, toeing the fallen pile of paper meaningfully.

'At least my book notes are useful, but I'm clearing those out too. Once they're all in the book, off to the recycling with the lot.'

Mum K scooped up a box marked *TWIN STUDIES*, and clanked down the ladder with it tucked under her arm.

Sammie knelt, carefully placing the pirate ship on one side and pulling out another smaller box. It was full of photographs – two small Sams on a beach, both buried up to their necks in sand; two bigger Sams dressed as two halves of a pumpkin for Halloween; baby Sams, one crooked in the arms of each mum – along with a notebook, *Sam and Sam: First Words* lovingly written on the cover, and a hand-drawn card, rather scribbled, with *HAPPY MOTHERS' DAY* in crayon, the apostrophe underlined twice.

Sammie stuck her head out of the trapdoor. 'Is she really going to throw us away?'

'No!' said Mum Gen.

'Yes!' shouted Mum K, at exactly the same time. She gave Mum Gen a stern look. 'Come on, we agreed. We need a clear-out. A proper one.'

'Why?' asked Sam, blinking up from below.

Mum Gen and Mum K grinned at one another, at exactly the same time: one of those secret-sharing grown-up smiles.

'Oi!' yelled Sammie. 'You're not allowed to have secrets! House rules!'

Mum K was a firm believer in treating children like adults – which meant no secrets, no vague promises to do something 'one day' when really that meant 'no', and no kind pretending that Pogle the hamster had *gone to sleep*; no, Pogle was stiff and cold and buried in the garden in a Carr's Table Water biscuits box. Mum Gen, meanwhile, was an equally firm believer in hamster heaven.

But Mum K clanked back up the ladder without a word.

Mum Gen tapped the side of her nose, smiling annoyingly – until the doorbell rang and made her jump.

'Oh crikey. Time for the New Routine to begin!'

And she hurried off to welcome Mr and Mrs Stravinksi (marital strife) onto the golden sofa.

3

SECRET #2:

JUST AS SUPERMAN IS VULNERABLE TO
KRYPTONITE, CAPTAIN SAMAZING'S POWERS
VANISH IN THE PRESENCE OF HUMMUS

TREETOPS HOMEWORK QUIZ!
*This homework quiz is private. You
don't have to share it with anyone
except Miss Townie.*

My name is: SAM PAGET-
SKIDELSKY (THE BOY ONE)
My age is: ll
My best friends are: PEA (FROM NEXT
DOOR TO MY HOUSE, NOT SCHOOL)

ALL OF OTTERS TABLE (NISHAT AND HONEY AND OLIVER BAXTER AND LUANNA-BELLA)

HALID

ALFIE

CHRISTOPHER FROM ART CLUB

MISS TOWNIE

Foods I like to eat are: CHEESE SANDWICHES, GRAPES, SPAGHETTI, HAM, BANANAS, CHICKEN – BASICALLY ALL THE FOODS THAT ARE NOT HUMMUS

Foods I don't like to eat are: HUMMUS

Foods I'm not allowed to eat are: DOG BISCUITS?

I am looking forward to: LUNCH TIME.

I am worried about: WHAT IS IN MY LUNCH BOX. BECAUSE MUM K MADE OUR LUNCHES THIS MORNING AND I DON'T KNOW IF SHE KNOWS ABOUT ME AND HUMMUS SO IT MIGHT BE IN MY SANDWICHES INSTEAD OF CHEESE.

Is there anything else you would like your teacher to know?

'That's not what that question means,' whispered Nishat, walking round the Otters table to collect up the homework.

Sam frowned. It had seemed a bit odd. In fact, the whole Treetops Homework Quiz had seemed a bit odd. Miss Townie already knew how much he liked cheese sandwiches; she was that sort of teacher. And what was a Treetops Homework Quiz anyway?

'What did *you* put?' he asked.

'Nothing,' said Nishat very quickly, keeping her own homework clamped tightly to her chest.

Sam fetched his *Stranger Danger* poster out of his tray. It was last week's art project, but Miss Townie said Sam could have extra time to finish due to his 'lovely attention to detail'. On Sam's *Stranger Danger* poster, Captain Samazing was rescuing a little girl from a Terrible Kidnapper. Or he would be, once Sam had added that bit; at the moment it was mostly squids, tiny robot unicorns, etc.

Gradually Class Six filled up: the Otters table, Sharks, Sticklebacks, Dragonflies and Herons. (The

25

Sharks were the Natterjack Toads table really. But when Sammie had written *SHARK NOM-NOM-NOM* and drawn a big toothy shark eating the Natterjack Toad on their table name instead, Miss Townie said it was 'a valuable learning opportunity' and made her teach everyone why Sharks do not live in *Streams & Rivers*. After that it had sort of stuck.)

Sam felt a strange hush of excitement in the air while Miss Townie took the register.

'Who did you put as your best friends?' whispered Nishat across the Otters table, anxiously eyeing the crumply pile of homework on Miss Townie's desk.

'I put you,' Honey whispered back.

'Me too.'

'And I put Luanna-Bella and Justina and Reema and Emily, in case there are six people sharing each room. Just to be definitely sure we won't be with—'

Sam was quite busy drawing the Terrible Kidnapper's hat, but he noticed them shooting the Sharks table a wary look, then looking apologetically back at him.

Sammie was slumped down in her chair, fiddling with her banana hair-clip, her cheeks pink. Reema and Emily (who was new, so had no idea she was actually a Natterjack Toad) sat  side by side next to her, whispering. They had hair-clips too: red cherries, both the same.

Girls were weird.

Nishat sighed. 'I wish I'd thought of that. Who did you put, Sam?'

Sam gave the Terrible Kidnapper a jaggedy scar and a big bushy beard. 'Loads of people. All of you, and Halid, and—'

Nishat and Honey burst out in giggles.

'You can't put us, you prawn,' said Honey. 'Didn't you read the letter you had to take home? Girls and boys aren't allowed to share at Treetops.'

'What's Treetops?'

They giggled even more.

Then Miss Townie turned on the smartboard. It said:

TREETOPS ACTIVITY CENTRE
Year 6 Summer Residential

There was a photograph of last year's Class Six underneath, all waving their arms in the air and smiling in some sort of forest.

Sam sat up straighter. He remembered now . . . There'd been a letter home that Mum Gen had signed, and a brown envelope with a cheque in it.

'Yes, you lucky things,' said Miss Townie, shushing

them with her hands as everyone began to whisper and scrape their chairs on the floor. 'It's almost here: Class Six's last big adventure before you all vanish off to Big School. Your chance to finally, truly get to know each other. It's our week-long residential. In just three weeks, believe it or not, you lot will be doing all this!'

Then the smartboard showed a montage of photos, still in the forest place, of last year's Class Six being brave and adventurous and extremely superheroic.

There was a climbing wall, hundreds of metres high like a cliff.

'*Oooh*,' said Christopher.

'Oh,' said Sam.

There were horses, and people sitting on them, far off the ground.

'*Horses*,' whispered Honey.

'Er,' said Sam.

There were giant trees with ropes slung between them, impossibly high up.

'*Whoa*,' breathed Luanna-Bella.

'Well,' said Sam.

There was even a video of Miss Townie in her

PE clothes, climbing up a ladder to a wooden platform surrounded by trees. (You could tell it was last year, because she had much shorter hair, and no sticky-out bump where she was growing a baby. She'd pinned a picture of the baby scan on the Class Six News Board. Class Six thought it looked more like a dinosaur than a baby, but she'd promised them it definitely wasn't one.)

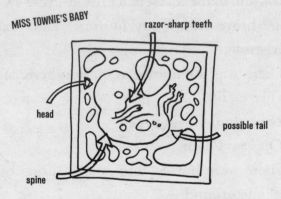

MISS TOWNIE'S BABY
razor-sharp teeth
head
possible tail
spine

'You'll like this,' said the real Miss Townie, to gasps, and she held up crossed fingers and grinned.

Sam gripped his pencil tightly, his hand all sweaty. The Miss Townie on the video held up crossed fingers and grinned too. Then she reached up and took hold of a tiny wooden bar attached to a rope stretched out between the tall trees. There was a long pause. Then she stepped off the edge of the platform and slid down along the rope – and she screamed and screamed all the time she was sliding, but the video stopped before you even got to see if she reached the other side.

'*Wowwww!*' said everyone.

But Sam didn't say anything at all. He was too busy gripping the pencil, and breathing, and wondering why there was a cold prickle of sweat sliding down his spine like a slug.

'That one's called the DEATH SLIDE OF DOOM!' said Miss Townie, with a beaming smile. 'And trust me: every single one of you is going to give it a try.'

4

Dear Reema,

Do you like javelining?

I bet you would if you tried it. You could come over next weekend or after school and we could javelin together.

I would give you half a Kit-Kat if you did.

By the way I saw Jade Johnson's sister last week and she says none of the Year Sevens at Kensal Rise High wear cherries in their hair. I hear the banana is considered the hair fruit of choice for the discerning pre-teen.

From your Best Friend,
Sammie

At packed lunch, Sammie sat by herself in the Reading Nook, dropping purposeful crumbs on Miss Townie's *Summery Stories* display. (It was made of sand glued to a piece of yellow cardboard, with boggly-eyed plastic starfish hanging on seaweed above it. You had to feel bad for that dinosaur baby growing inside her; its mother was clearly very confused about what actual human children liked. Sammie had no intention of ever having babies – *urgh* – though she wouldn't mind if it turned out to be a dinosaur. A good one, though; not a pterodactyl or something.)

Everyone else sat at the Otters and the Sharks tables as usual, and the talk was – of course – all Treetops.

Nishat was afraid of bees.

Luanna-Bella was scared everyone else would bring more pocket money than her.

Honey had to sleep with a special night-light on, because she was scared of the dark.

But the boys . . .

OK, Paolo – who had swoopy hair and a girl-friend and already used manly-smelling deodorant spray – confessed he sleepwalked, and might need to be fetched before he wandered melodramatically into the woods at midnight and fell in a pond.

But the rest? Oh no, they weren't worried about anything, not at all, not even a bit.

Not Alfie, who everyone knew only ate white bread and ketchup and would probably starve.

Not Oliver Baxter, who was allergic to everything.

Not Halid, who only had one hand and was going to a place where not everyone was maybe quite so used to it and knew not to stare.

Not her brother.

Poor Sam. Poor, rubbish, not-the-Best-Twin Sam, peeling his sandwiches apart and looking sickly.

And none of them even seemed to appreciate her pointing out, loudly, from the Reading Nook, that pretending you weren't scared was loads less brave than actually admitting it.

Boys were weird.

'Well, what are you scared of, then?' shouted Halid.

'Duh. Nothing.' She leaned out through the gap in the bookcases. 'You get to stay up all night with, like, no parents to tell you to go to sleep. You do actual galloping on horses and fencing with real swords. And Jade Johnson's sister said you go to a farm and stroke ducks and hold chickens. Only a total muppet would be scared of Treetops.'

A ripple of unhappiness circled Class Six – dispelled at once when Miss Townie sailed in, carrying a bundle of posters in her arms.

She ignored Sammie – *But crumbs, miss, I'm dropping so many crumbs on your special nook* – and pinned up the posters, twittering cheerfully about how Treetops had remarkably few bees, an extensive menu with many choices and clear allergy labelling, and reminding them all of the pocket money guidelines that would be going out in the next parental letter.

'Football?' suggested Alfie.

The Otters table emptied.

Sammie's feet twitched. Once upon a time Reema and Sammie always played football at lunch break. They were almost always the only girls, but if anyone dared suggest two of Kensal Rise Kites FC's star players weren't good enough to join in, Sammie would shout, 'I'm going to kick you in the knickers!' until they gave up.

But now Reema and Emily stayed in their seats, cherry hairclips clicking together as they whispered – about what? Swishy hair? Buttoning up all the pearly buttons on your grey school cardigan? It was mystifying; they did it all the time and it was just mystifying.

Sammie stayed in the Reading Nook. Reema would get bored soon. She would come over and ask what brilliant thing Sammie was doing, and she could show off exactly how many crumbs she'd made.

Miss Townie's round smiling face appeared over the top of the bookshelf. 'I don't seem to have had your Treetops Quiz, Sammie, my lovely. Did it get left at home, perhaps? Because I could just give you a new one to fill in, now, immediately. Hmm?' She produced a fresh sheet and a pen, still innocently smiling.

Sammie sighed, pulled a scrumpled ball of paper out of her pocket, and passed it up, not bothering to look apologetic.

TREETOPS HOMEWORK QUIZ!
This homework quiz is private. You don't have to share it with anyone except Miss Townie.

My name is: SAMMIE – NOT SAM

My age is: 11

My best friends are: is Reema.
You can only have one BEST friend. You are a teacher,
miss, I think you should know that
already.

Foods I like to eat are: Fudge,
Kettle Chips, the middle bit out of custard
creams

Foods I don't like to eat are:
Butternut squash

Foods I'm not allowed to eat are:
Pine needles

I am looking forward to: ALL OF
TREETOPS
Especially no mums
Staying up all night telling ghost stories with my best
friend
Horse-riding
Archery
Zip-wires
Danger
Being better than everyone at everything

I am worried about: Nothing

Only a total muppet would be worried about
Treetops
**Is there anything else you would
like your teachers to know?**
This isn't really a quiz, is it, miss?

Miss Townie read it twice.

Sammie waited to get told off – *Yes, miss, I am being
a bit rude, I'm like that, that's why I'm fun and funny and a
totally brilliant best friend* – but instead Miss Townie
tilted her head to one side and said, 'Oh, Sammie.
Believe it or not, I'm going to miss you next year.'

And she sailed away, as if crumbs didn't matter
to her at all.

That evening, Sam was lying on his stripy bedroom
rug, deep in tentacles. Surprise was gnawing the leg
of Sam's bed while Sammie leaned against Sam's
bedroom door, fussing with her now fruit-less hair.

Mum Gen waved off her last unhappy person of
the day (Mrs Bishop: nervous flier), and came up the
stairs to find them.

'Oof, what a day,' she said, unpinning her hair

from its knot and flopping back onto his bed with a bounce. 'I even had to go and buy a new box of tissues at lunch time to keep up with all those extra-sad people. Hello, silly dog. Come here, you two. Tell me happy things! Cheer me up!'

When Mum Gen walked them home from school, she always asked how their day had been, in a Professionally Gentle way. Mum K hadn't seemed to know about that bit. Which was probably lucky, since Sammie had been given three sad clouds on the whiteboard for talking to Reema, passing notes to Reema, and hitting Reema on the forehead with a shatterproof ruler. (Miss Townie had given Reema a smiley face for 'being sensible enough to ignore her'.)

Mum Gen wasn't going to find any of it very up-cheering.

'Well. Oliver Baxter sat on Honey's purple gel pen and got glittery pants,' said Sam, flopping onto the bed too.

'Oh dear. Poor Oliver Baxter.'

'Luanna-Bella fell asleep in Literacy and we only noticed because she snored and fell off her chair,' Sammie added, sinking onto the stripy rug.

Mum Gen giggled.

'And . . .'

'Um . . .'

Sam looked at Sammie.

Sammie looked at Sam.

That was the thing about being twins. There was always one person who knew exactly what you were thinking, without you saying a word.

'Nothing else,' said Sammie lightly.

'Nothing at all,' said Sam. 'Tell us about your day.'

And Mum Gen did, for ages, while Sam looked at his ceiling and thought emphatically about tiny robot unicorns, and Spidey, and nothing OF DOOM at all.

5

Dear Mum K,

Your book is completely wrong and stupid already and you're only on page 3.

Also you have a bit too much Sam in it for a book that is about me.

You should probably set fire to it and start all over again. Here are some matches.

From Sammie

Dear Sammie,

Thanks for the charming editorial input. I might quote this letter in Chapter 2. (No, you won't be paid a royalty.) Are you allowed matches?

K

You are a mum — you are supposed to know if I'm allowed matches.

'Breakfast all together on a school day again — what a treat,' said Mum Gen brightly, yawning as she buttered her toast. 'Although, Sammie dear — I know her sparkling morning conversation may have made this hard to spot, but Mum K does live with us all the time now. She's that dead-looking person sitting at the other end of the breakfast table. You don't actually need to write her letters any more.'

'She wrote back! Anyway, she likes my letters.'

Sammie knew she did. Mum K had kept them all; they were in a box in the attic held together with an elastic band, with the best bits highlighted in green pen.

Mum K grunted, her nose buried deep in her coffee cup.

'You write letters to Mum K?' asked Sam, blinking over his bowl of Cheerios.

'Every week. Or I did. See? I am totally, definitely the Best Twin.'

'How many times! There's no such thing as the Best Twin,' said Mum Gen, aggressively buttering more toast.

'There is, and I am it. And I *am* nice. And thoughtful, and considerate.'

'Who said you weren't?'

'*She* did!' said Sammie, thrusting a typed sheet of paper onto Mum Gen's crumby plate.

INTRODUCTION – page 3

While it was never our intention for the twins' gender identity to be a mystery, we rapidly learned that having a child named 'Sam' allowed adults and other children to draw their own conclusions – sometimes wrongly – and this began to reveal a pattern.

If either Sam played with trains or pushed a child off a swing, they were assumed to be a boy.

If either Sam carried a doll or said Duh 'please', they were assumed to be a girl.

43

Sometimes we'd let it slide. Sometimes we would smile and gently say, 'Actually, that Sam's a girl,' or 'this Sam's a boy' – and usually the response would be a rueful shrug. (Sometimes, I must confess, we lied, just to be annoying.) But as the children grew older and spent more time out of the house, in social situations, we heard a different response.

'You should cut his hair – it's very confusing.'

'I wouldn't dress a boy in pink – he might turn out . . . y' know.'

'She can't have that one – that's for boys.'

At first this piqued my interest from a purely clinical perspective. But as time went by we began to wonder what messages our children were absorbing about their behaviour, their personalities, their hopes and dreams.

It wasn't a problem for us, but it seemed that a hard-to-pin-down 'Sam' was a problem for other people. Suddenly complete strangers would be rude, even unkind, to our children in

Handwritten margin notes:
Why am I not allowed to be annoying if you are allowed to be annoying?

That one is stupid though you should ignore those people

So we changed their names to Jonathan and Charlotte instead and it was all fixed the end

44

somewhere as innocuous as a playground or a library.

Now that we have two eleven-year-olds, their distinct personalities and character traits stand out starkly. (Throughout the text the two children will be referred to as Sam A and Sam B, with no personal pronouns used to indicate gender.)

Sam A is bold, rebellious and creative. Quick-witted, confident and assertive, Sam A has leadership qualities and an adventurous spirit. A prefers to be the centre of attention, and sometimes struggles to comprehend a situation from another's point of view. Life for Sam A is a series of challenges to be conquered and battles to be fought, sometimes with shouting.

Sam B, by contrast, is one of life's observers. B does not need or desire to be the centre of attention, and would rather take the equally valuable role of 'second-in-command', sidekick, team player – although B is also highly self-motivated and task-oriented, preferring to focus quietly on a single

45

```
activity until it is completed. Sam B is
sensible, rational, thoughtful and considerate.
```
this book
is awful

'Oh dear,' said Mum Gen, frowning as she read.

'I did not!' said Mum K, reaching over to snatch the paper. 'I said Sam A was . . . *confident and assertive*. Which seems to be true, since you've asserted yourself all over my margins.'

'And you said Sam B was thoughtful and considerate! Which means you don't think I'm thoughtful and considerate – or you would've said I was too.'

'Interesting. How do you know Sam A is you?'

'Duh. Because it's obvious.'

'There you go!' Mum K took off her glasses and polished them, looking from twin to twin thoughtfully. 'Now – Gen's right, there's no such thing as the Best Twin. But you are different. Being honest, Sammie – you know I always try to be honest – I think you'd admit that you're assertive and bold more often than you're thoughtful and considerate, wouldn't you? And Sam here is a quieter, gentler soul: sensible, calm—'

'What?' said Sam.

Sammie plucked the page disgustedly from Mum Gen's hands and gave it to him to read.

Sam nodded slowly. 'No, Sammie, I'm Sam A – you've got them mixed up,' he said; then 'Oh . . .'; then '*Oh . . .*' – and then he put the paper down, looking vaguely sick. 'A sidekick,' he whispered.

'I know,' said Sammie, shaking her head sadly. 'And she's missed out all my niceness, and how I am an excellent best friend. Your book is awful, Mum K.' Really, it would have to be set on fire.

'It's a joy to be working from home, truly,' said Mum K, downing her coffee.

Sam frowned at the single Cheerio swimming in his spoon. 'Were people really mean to us in the park when we were tiny?'

Mum Gen rubbed her eyes. 'Oh, not mean, exactly. Sometimes they were confused. Two Sams in the same family is rather unusual. Much more unusual than two mums, and some people were already quite confused about that.'

'Why *did* you call us both Sam, though?' asked Sammie. 'Because – it is not very normal. At all.'

Jonathan and Charlotte. Those were good names.

No one would be horrible to Jonathan and Charlotte in a park.

'We've told you a thousand times,' said Mum Gen. 'We both liked the name, that's all. When you have babies, you spend ages thinking of names, the best names . . .' She paused, fiddling with the crust of her toast.

'Gen,' said Mum K, very softly.

Mum Gen brightened suddenly, jumping up to poke through the pile of files and books and papers on the side. 'Hold on, I can show you. I thought this was lost years ago, but it was in one of those dusty old boxes . . . Aha!'

She produced a crumpled sheet of handwritten names on paper so worn it had gone slightly furry. There were two lists: one in Mum K's scribbly hand-writing, one in Mum Gen's tidier slanted script beside it.

Rocky	Simon
Zorro	Anna
Jolene	Penelope
Tilda	Tristan
Jupiter	Ella

Ajax	Remus
Jack	William
Sam	Sam
Bill	Adeline
Sirius	Paul/Pauline
Julien	Juliette

'Haha! All right, Ajax Paget-Skidelsky.' Sammie gave Sam a nudge with her elbow.

But Mum Gen was jabbing her finger at the page triumphantly. 'See? Only one name on both lists. It was the only one we could agree on, for months and months. And we kept on saying, *We'll think of more, we'll think of more*, but . . . Baby names are hard, you know – you want to choose a perfect one and . . . you'll be living with that name for ever, and – well . . .'

'Gen,' said Mum K again, in a voice that was very nearly Professionally Gentle. 'Do you think . . . now might be the time?'

Mum Gen stood very still, her hand still resting on the list of names, fingers spread out to touch *Tilda* and *Jack* and *Remus*, an odd smile on her face.

'Time for what?' Sammie demanded. They were doing it again. That secretive thing.

But then the doorbell rang, and Mum Gen coughed, and tucked wisps of hair behind her ears, and brushed crumbs off her tummy – the round bit, where it stuck out over the top of her skirt – and hurried away to welcome to the golden sofa Ms Barandhophay and her fear of bats.

6

Class Six had an unhappy Tuesday.

Oliver Baxter chewed the end of his biro and painted his lips, tongue and teeth quite blue.

Alfie gave Halid a black eye while trying to teach him how to fake-punch people like in films.

Sammie was given three sad clouds on the white-board for sitting on Reema, pulling Reema's hair, and climbing under the table and gluing herself to Reema's ankle. (Emily spent all of Literacy picking dried glue-gunk out of the holey pattern in her left knee sock, tutting.)

And Sam . . .

Sam was not himself.

The Terrible Kidnapper drawing kept coming out of the end of his pencil all wrong.

He played Animal Habitats with Honey and accidentally made all her polar bears live in a desert. ('They're dead,' she said. 'You polar-bear murderer.')

And the last hour of the day was spent in the hall with the dreaded Mrs McMin, Deputy Head, who was in charge of the impending Class Six Leavers' Assembly. Mrs McMin hated all children, but the Sams especially. They were too alike ('As if!' said Mum

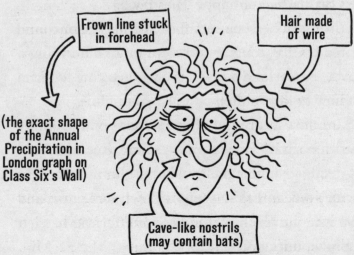

DREADED MRS MCMIN

Frown line stuck in forehead

Hair made of wire

(the exact shape of the Annual Precipitation in London graph on Class Six's Wall)

Cave-like nostrils (may contain bats)

Gen) and too confusing (which he really wasn't; he was just Sam) and a terrible distraction (when all he was doing was sitting on his chair). The year the twins had spent in her class had not been a happy one: Sam had spent most of it being wrongfully accused of pen theft, glue-based crime and knicker-kicking, before Mrs McMin bore down with her enormous nostrils and bellowed, 'Wait – which one are you again?'

At the Leavers' Assembly, everyone was supposed to show off a talent or a skill. Paolo, Alfie and Halid were doing some sort of complicated dance. Nell was going to play the tuba. Sammie had threatened to 'demonstrate the javelin'. But *Captain Samazing versus the Mermaid Apocalypse* was declared 'lacking in literary merit' – so instead of reading Sam found himself commanded to stand on a chair and sing a solo of *For Those in Peril on the Sea* while Mrs McMin thumped wildly at the piano.

The words were on a piece of paper in front of him, but he didn't know the tune, and anyway his head kept filling up unhelpfully with the sound of Miss Townie's screams as she swung down and down and down into the black nothingness OF DOOM . . .

'Sing louder, you silly girl!' shouted Mrs McMin.

Everyone laughed. Even Halid. Even Christopher and Nishat and all his best-friend list at Treetops.

'Not that there's anything *wrong* with being a girl,' said Sammie later as they waited in the playground after school.

'No,' said Sam with a heavy sigh. 'But I'm not one.'

When Mum K arrived to collect them, she was wearing a neon-orange vest, neon-green shorts, and trainers with neon-pink stripes. Sam could just see a flash of blue-streaked hair under a neon-yellow cap.

'Why are you dressed as a complete set of highlighter pens?' he asked.

Mum K bounced on her toes and windmilled her arms. 'Just done a brisk five k around the park. Used to run back from the office every day, back in Edinburgh; need to keep up the habit. Good for the heart. And the dog.'

Surprise gave a sharp bark of disapproval, then lay down and dribbled aggressively all over Mum K's trainer.

'Horrifying,' said Sammie, marching out of the

school gates with her school bag on her head in case anyone saw.

'Now then, you two: what do you remember about being seven?'

'Why?'

'For my book, of course! Can't find my notes for that year. Besides, I'm curious about what you recall most clearly yourselves, without stimuli – no photographs, no adult prompts. There could be a whole chapter on conflicting memories in families. That's why twins are such *fascinating* clinical resources . . .'

Sam endeavoured to be a fascinating clinical resource. They'd gone to Pizza Express for their seventh birthday party – even though Sam had thought it would be Pizza Hut. They might have had a holiday with Grandma Paget, somewhere hot and beachy (he'd got sunburn all over his shoulders and his skin had peeled off in white bits, like the pith off an orange) – but that could easily have been the year before.

Sammie could only remember the time the Tooth Fairy forgot to come. (She'd come back the following night, with under-the-pillow excuses, but from the look on Sammie's face she was still in disgrace.)

Dear Sam,

I am dreadfully sorry for the delayed collection of your tooth. This was due to one of your mothers VERY FOOLISHLY not believing in fairies, so she didn't leave it under your pillow for me to find. Fortunately your other mother is much more sensitive, and kindly left me clear directions. What a lovely tooth! Thank you. Here is a pound.

With love from
The Tooth Fairy

They were still arguing about it when they got home.

'For the last time, Sammie: there is no Dog Tooth Fairy! What would a dog do with a pound anyway? Oh, hang on,

wait here – I have *got* to talk to that nice woman in a hard hat.'

Sam froze.

'*No, don't go over there,*' hissed Sammie.

But it was too late. Mum K was already pressing Surprise's lead into Sam's hand, and jogging across the road.

To the Bad House.

It was number 27 really. But everyone knew it was the Bad House. It was a tall, solitary house of red bricks, set back a little from the road in the shadow of a big tree. The windows were boarded up with black metal plates. There were gaps in the slates on the roof where some had fallen in. The drive was all tufty grass growing up through cracks in the concrete, and brambles. Grown-ups tutted and sighed about *lowering the tone* and *lowering their house prices,* but anyone with any sense was much more worried about the *Bad Man* who so obviously lived in the *Bad House,* and the terrible howling, moaning screams that came from inside late at night.

Sam had never actually heard any screams, though they lived almost directly opposite. In fact, Sam had never met anyone who had heard the

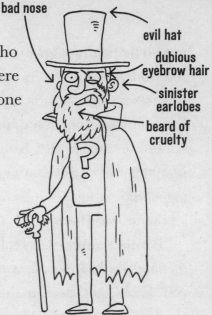

bad nose

evil hat

dubious
eyebrow hair

sinister
earlobes

beard of
cruelty

screams; only people who
were quite sure that there
had been some. And no one
had ever seen the Bad
Man, or knew what he
looked like (though Sam
had a very clear picture
in his head, which
he was sure must've
come from some-
where). Still, the
Bad House looked very
believably haunted and horrible. Sam had loosely
planned to vanquish him, heroically, in a not-at-all
sidekick-like fashion, when he finally showed up.

But apparently he'd have to hurry: soon the Bad
Man would have to find a new place to live. The Bad
House now had a Heavenly Construction van parked
on the crumbly concrete, a yellow skip, and three
levels of scaffolding being added to its scary blank-
eyed face.

Over on the other side of the road, Mum K chat-
ted to one of the builders: a woman with a blonde
ponytail and a dusty red-and-blue checked shirt. She

waved her arms vaguely towards their house, sketching something in the air: a zigzag, and some sort of tugging motion. Mum K nodded, and waggled her fingers up and down mysteriously. The other builder – an old man with leathery tanned skin and a blond ponytail too – was up on the second level of scaffolding, sliding a ladder into position so he could climb all the way to the top.

Surprise nibbled on Sam's ankle as he watched the leathery builder climb, and climb, and climb.

That slithery slug of fear slid down his spine again.

'It's a very long way up, that ladder,' said Sammie, suddenly standing close beside him, breathing on his neck.

'Is it?' said Sam, very casually.

'Or a very long way down, depending on how you look at it.'

'Suppose so.'

'Probably about the same height as that DEATH SLIDE OF DOOM at Treetops.'

Sam shivered, all over.

'Sam.'

'It's just hummus,' he blurted. 'That's all! Bit of cheese, I'll be fine!'

Sammie stepped in front of him, and his eyes met her clear, critical brown ones.

'It's not hummus,' she said.

That was the thing about being a twin. There was always someone who knew you, exactly. Someone who'd noticed you'd never been up the ladder into the attic in your own house. Someone who knew that you'd tried and only ever got as far as rung number four before the world spun and tilted and it was necessary to have a bit of a lie down.

'It's not hummus,' Sam repeated faintly as the leathery builder clambered across the rooftop, and the slug went on creeping down his back.

He was scared of Treetops. Of ladders. Of high trees and the DEATH SLIDE OF DOOM.

More than scared.

And that was the most frightening thing of all, because Sam Paget-Skidelsky, the boy one, wasn't meant to be scared of anything.

7

Dear Nishat/Honey/Luanna-Bella/
Justina/Grace (delete as appropriate),

A vacancy has unexpectedly opened up for the
position of Best Friend of Sammie
Paget-Skidelsky.

We expect there to be a great deal of
competition for this enticing role, as Sammie is
brilliant, funny, exciting and the Best Twin.
Apply immediately to avoid disappointment!

Signed,
The Official Bureau of Best-Friendship

'It's OK, Sam,' said Sammie, reassuringly patting his arm. 'I won't tell anyone you're completely pathetic.'

Sam just went on staring up at the ladder as if it might javelin him in the face any second.

Poor Sam, she thought. It had to be hard, being the rubbish twin.

Outside the Bad House, the check-shirted builder shook Mum K's hand with her grubby glove, and Mum K zipped back across the road with a smile.

'How handy is that? Need a builder and, as if by magic, one appears right over the road!'

'Why do we need a builder?'

'Mm? Oh. Well . . .' Mum K gave a little cough and adjusted her glasses. 'You know how it is – lots of little jobs around the house piling up over the years. Never found the time when I was away . . .' And she smiled a tight, secretive little smile.

'House rules!' shouted Sammie. 'Remember? No secrets allowed!'

But Mum K was already striding down the side passage into the garden instead of opening the front door, so as not to disturb any of Mum Gen's unhappy people.

Beside the back door sat a pottery fox, sitting up with its nose pointed to the sky and its brushy tail coiled over its paws. Mum K tilted it, and plucked a small silver key from the dry patch of patio underneath. She let them in, and dropped the key back under the fox.

'Go on – homework! I'll bring you a drink in a second.'

Surprise sniffled at the floor, then went scampering ahead, letting out a series of excited barks.

Sammie followed, dragging her school bag along the floor into the study, making scrapy noises – then stopped so sharply that Sam walked right into her.

'Ow! What are you— Oh!'

The study was not a big room, and it always had quite a lot of things in it: an upright piano, a dining table with four heavy wooden chairs, two bookcases, a fireplace and mantelpiece cluttered with photos in frames and vases. But today it also contained:

- Mum K's book research, in orderly piles of paper, notebooks and photos on the dining table

- stacks of dusty attic cardboard boxes
  with handwritten labels – *SAM & SAM:
  6–12 MONTHS* or *NOTES: LANGUAGE
  ACQUISITION* or *HOSPITAL* – piled up
  in every corner
- a small boy

It was all quite surprising, but the small boy especially so. Sammie guessed he was probably about eight. He had smooth brown skin and shiny black hair, like Reema and Nishat at school, and he was wearing a school uniform, though the top was white, not yellow like theirs. He sat at the far end of the table, holding a pencil in his fist like a weapon, as their excited puppy bounced up against his knee.

'Are you allowed to be in here?' asked Sammie, thumping her bag down hard on the table and scooping Surprise into her arms before there could be a dribbling incident.

The boy narrowed his eyes, still brandishing the pencil. He licked his lips. But he didn't say anything.

'Um,' said Sam. 'She's not being rude, she just means that this is our house. We live in it. And you don't, so that's why we're a bit startled. I'm Sam.'

The boy licked his lips again.

'And she's Sammie,' Sam added helpfully. 'This is Surprise.'

Surprise barked, and shook out his mould-green ears.

Still silence.

Marvellous. Sammie spent all day at school stuck with boys being weird, and now there was a new one in her own house, sitting in her chair and being weird in it.

'This is the bit where you say what your name is,' she said. 'Do you not know how to have conversations?'

The boy made a sort of gulping sound, like a sigh had got stuck in his throat – but he still said nothing.

'Sorry, should have done the introductions first,' said Mum K, striding in with a tray with three glasses of lemon squash. 'This is Rohan. Mr Grover – that's his dad – is just next door with Gen, and they needed to talk about a few things in private, so Rohan's come to sit with us, haven't you?'

The boy said nothing, but he lowered the pencil just a fraction.

Mum K flashed him a big smile. 'Sam and Sammie are going to sit very quietly in here with us and get on with some homework. OK with you, Rohan?'

The boy nodded.

And that was how they spent the next half-hour: squashed in tight around the table in the cramped little room with a strange quiet hanging in the air. Mum K tapped away on her laptop. Sam did some maths puzzles. Sammie turned the pages of *The Secret Life of the English Hedgerow* at I-might-plausibly-have-read-this-by-now intervals, and poked through old photos.

Sams at their third birthday party. (Sammie's eyes were closed, blowing out the candles. Sam was still drawing a breath).

Sams squished together in one cot, asleep, dressed in matching green and red onesies. (Sammie was the one in red, probably. Biggest, taking up the most space.)

Sams before they were born inside Mum K's huge planet belly. (Mum K's hair was faded pink Mostly she stared at Rohan.

It wasn't as if she wanted a new friend. She had a best friend, a Reema-shaped best friend; Reema who used to love being hit on the head with a shatterproof ruler, and would probably enjoy javelining, if she would only talk to Sammie long enough to be invited. And this Rohan was a boy, and small, and sort of weird. But Sammie wouldn't have minded a sparc, for emergencies.

And, quite unfairly, Sam seemed to be making friends with him without even trying.

He was drawing some kind of squid things on his comic.

And the weird silent boy watched him, then turned his stabby pencil round and began to draw them too, on his own piece of paper.

Sam smiled.

Rohan smiled back.

Sammie smiled as well – but of course they didn't notice. She tried doodling a squid on the corner of Mum K's *Introduction*, but it came out with its legs all wrong, and she scribbled it out before they could see.

Once he'd run out of tentacle space, Rohan turned his page over, sucked the end of the pencil, then started drawing again. He kept one hand curled over his page and his head bent very low while he

was working, but when he sat up Sammie could see
the whole picture: a house, neatly drawn with
curtains at each window, a cat on the front step, and
a little curl of smoke coming from the chimney.

'Cool,' said Sam. 'You're really good at drawing,
Rohan.'

Rohan's mouth curved up into a shy smile.

'And I like your' – Sammie scanned him up
and down urgently – 'pencil. It's very . . . well
sharpened.'

The shy smile faded at once.

Mum K blinked at Sammie over her laptop, then
peered at the picture. 'Interesting,' she said. 'Did you
know, Rohan, that if presented with a blank sheet of

paper and asked to draw anything at all, the vast majority of people draw a house?'

Rohan's nose crinkled up, as if he didn't know that, and hadn't especially wanted to.

'One just like that,' Mum K continued, 'with a winding path and smoke coming out of a chimney – when who has a working fireplace these days? The cat is unusual, though; a more personal touch.'

Rohan, now looking rather besieged, tucked the house drawing away and began to draw something else on a new sheet, still without saying a word.

'*I* think,' announced Sammie, shuffling importantly in her seat, 'that—' – but a stare from Mum K made her stop. 'I was only going to say I liked the cat too,' she muttered.

She went on reading Mum K's stupid Introduction, and felt crosser and crosser.

Eventually there was a rap at the door, and Mum Gen peeped in.

'Thanks for being so patient, Rohan! Your dad's all ready to go now.'

There was a man in the hall behind her:

Rohan's dad, Sammie supposed, Mr Grover. Most of Mum K's unhappy people looked sort of stringy and red-eyed after an hour on her golden sofa (Sammie had been home poorly the day Mr Peck had wept long past his allotted time, and a small queue had formed in the hallway, all sniffs and clutched tissues, waiting for their go) – but not Mr Grover. He was  brown like Rohan, but his black hair was impeccably slicked back, apart from one stray curl across his forehead, and he wore a tight white shirt, with enormous bulging arm muscles like a series of hourglasses, and big chesty ones, like boobs, but manly. His eyes were bright, and he flashed them a grin, showing perfect straight white teeth.

Surprise bounded up to him at once, and dribbled on his trainer with instant affection.

Sammie couldn't blame him; she found herself sitting up straight and smiling and hoping he'd shake her hand hello – though she had no idea why. He just seemed good, somehow; good, and kind, and not built to be unhappy.

Mr Grover reached down to ruffle Surprise's ears fondly. 'All right, Ro, mate? You all set?' he said, in a slightly unexpected Australian accent.

Rohan edged out from behind all the boxes and, on his way to the door, handed Sam his drawing.

Sammie leaned over to see.

It was a house again – but not like the first one. Instead of a curvy path and a curly-smoked chimney, this was a wide blocky building with only one storey, like a bungalow. There was a swimming pool in the garden, with chairs around it. On one chair sat a cat, curled up, just like in the other picture.

Hi Sam,
You're really good at drawing too.
This is a picture of my REAL house.
Rohan

'You've got a swimming pool?' said Sammie, looking Rohan up and down again. She could totally put up with a weird silent boy for a friend if he had a swimming pool, and a dad with manly boobs.

But Mr Grover plucked the picture off the table, shaking his head ruefully. 'Used to, more like. This is our old place, back in Melbourne.' He held the paper very tightly in his massive hands, a frown deepening in his forehead.

'How lovely,' said Mum Gen, in her Professionally Gentle voice. 'Perhaps next time you come, Rohan might like to draw the house you're living in now, hmm?'

Rohan's face went stiff, and he shuffled behind his dad, out of sight.

'Yeah, all right. Let's get going, eh? See if your mum's home yet? Thanks for keeping an eye on him, guys.'

Mr Grover slid the drawing back in front of Sam, flashed him another dazzling smile, and left.

8

INTRODUCTION - page 10

As parents and carers of the internet age,
most of us will have experienced the 'over-
share'. While this proliferation of proud
anecdotes and snapshots is presented as casual
public celebration amongst a supportive peer
network, it may also take on a competitive
edge. Whose child walked earliest? Whose child
is dry? If little Jaspreet can read already,
why can't my little Joseph?

Often, parents and carers perceive such
sharing to be a direct criticism of their own
parenting choices.

Why, then, would any couple - especially
one with our clinical experience - choose to
document the lives of their children so closely

What are you lking bout?

Who is?

You are just making people up now

This is a good question

in a book? Can my conclusions hold any professional value when I am so personally involved in both my interpretation of their behaviour, and the fostering of that behaviour in the first place? Is this simply an exercise in vanity? How have the years spent knowingly compiling this material influenced the way we have parented our children? And how do Sam A and Sam B feel about their lives being placed in public view?

No they can'

You should stop writing thi boo" Mum K

We would like to se this book on fire

'Have you asked them?' asked Mum Gen, frowning over the pages at Friday morning breakfast.

'Naturally,' said Mum K frostily. 'Sammie wrote me a three-page letter documenting her feelings, which Sam signed – as well as adding a rather sweet drawing of a cat. I might include it in an appendix; it does provide quite a neat demonstration of their personalities . . .'

Sammie stabbed a knife into the butter.

Mum Gen's frown grew deeper.

Mum K rolled her eyes. 'Oh, shush. You can't be misunderstood yet, Sammie, you're not a teenager. Mercifully.'

But I am, Sammie thought. *I am the misunderstoodest.*

No matter how hard she tried, no one seemed to be remembering that she was the Best Twin: fun, and funny, and completely friendworthy.

Luanna-Bella did not appreciate being told her hair was 'the tangliest in the whole school'.

Honey didn't laugh when Sammie spent all of Class Six Leavers' Assembly practice doing an impression of Mrs McMin, complete with fingers in her nostrils.

And at the end of lunch, Oliver Baxter had to be carried to the nurse, bleeding, after an unfortunate nose-versus-football incident.

'I was trying to be Thoughtful and Considerate by not scoring any goals,' Sammie explained as Miss Townie drew a large sad cloud on the whiteboard, with a sigh. 'Only Oliver Baxter was goalie and he's useless – so I had to keep kicking it right at his face, just to make sure.'

Dear Oliver,

I'm sorry about your face. This was wrong because now your nose is all mushy. In future I will just score goals as usual.

All the while Emily Roche, with her buttoned-up cardigan and her swishable hair, sat smiling and innocent in Sammie's old chair.

'How do you do it, Sam?' Sammie asked at lunch time, sitting crumbily in the Reading Nook.

'What?'

'Make friends.'

Sam tapped his pencil thoughtfully on his chin. 'I don't know. Just . . . be nice?'

'I am nice!'

'Are you?'

'Yes!'

Sam looked doubtful.

When Mum K walked them home, she stopped opposite the Bad House.

'Go on in round the back, you two,' she said, swiftly crossing the road. 'Just need another chat with Angel there.'

The check-shirted builder from Heavenly Construction gave Mum K a wave from the top of the scaffolding, and began to climb down the grim, grimy face of the Bad House.

Sam's face turned pale.

Poor Sam. Poor not-the-Best-Twin Sam.

The twins let themselves in with the key from under the pottery fox.

In the study were yet more attic boxes, and Rohan again, sitting silently drawing.

Sammie glared at him instinctively – then remembered she was Thoughtful and Considerate and that he used to have a swimming pool, and grinned instead.

'Hello, Rohan! How are you today?' she said, in a strange, gravelly approximation of the Professionally Gentle voice.

Rohan recoiled, his eyes turning huge.

'Is your dad talking to my mum again?' She fluttered her eyelashes sympathetically.

Rohan slid sideways and hid his face behind a

box labelled *SAMS: LETTERS FROM GEN.*

'Would you like half a Kit-Kat?' Sammie said, leaning over and thrusting one – rather dusty, from rattling around in the bottom of her school bag – under his nose.

Rohan put his head under a sheet of paper.

Sam elbowed her sharply.

'Ow!'

'Stop it! Sorry, Rohan. Just ignore her.'

'I'm being nice!'

'Well, stop, 'cos you aren't any good at it!'

Mum K's voice floated up the hall. 'Come on through, Angel – yes, boots off, thank you.'

'No sweat. So – what sort of time frame did you have in mind?'

Sam and Sammie wrestled over a pencil case as two sets of feet thumped up the stairs – and then the door flew open.

Mum Gen's face was an unusual shade of pink. 'What on earth is going on in here?' she hissed. Then she smoothed down her hair and smiled. 'So sorry, Rohan. I didn't mean to leave you alone with these two.'

She removed the twins from the study, and sent

Rohan off to the golden sofa to sit with his dad. Then she glared at them in the hallway, one eyebrow raised.

'I was being friendly!' said Sammie, folding her arms poutily. 'I said hello and offered Rohan a Kit-Kat. And then Sam hit me with an elbow and sat on me.'

Sam opened his mouth to protest – then shrugged. 'Yeah. That is basically what happened.'

Mum Gen stared from twin to twin. She picked up a stray strand of Sammie's hair. 'Is it possible you've swapped heads?'

They both shook their heads firmly.

She stared a bit more, then groaned in defeat. 'Just don't tell Kara, or Chapter Six will have to go in the bin. Now be nice to each other!'

She disappeared back into the front room, saying, 'So sorry, Mr Grover,' in a very Professionally Gentle way.

There was a long mirror in the hall, where Mum Gen pinned her wisps of hair into a straggly bun every morning.

Sammie stared at their reflections.

'*Is* it possible?' whispered Sam, touching his face as if worried it might not be his.

They were twins, still. Sams, still. But not like the cutesy photos on the mantelpiece: two halves of a stripy-jumpered whole. It wasn't only the haircuts. Even in their matching yellow polo tops and grey uniform trousers, they hardly looked alike at all. Sammie had grown taller and wider. Sam's face was thinner and frecklier. No one could possibly mix them up now, even if they plucked off their heads and switched them like Lego.

And obviously it was brilliant, because Sammie was the tallest and he was a weed, she was so much the Best Twin it hurt, but . . .

When had that happened?

How?

Everything was changing, without anyone asking her if she wanted it to.

Mum K's voice floated down from upstairs, talking to Angel about the attic. Their attic, which *suddenly* needed to be emptied out; where there *suddenly* wouldn't be room for their old things ; where *suddenly* something – someone – more important needed to take up space . . .

The Sammie in the mirror stared back at her, her lips twisted up, angry and sad.

'Sam,' she said eventually. 'I know obviously Mum K's book is awful and really ought to be set on fire, but – what if she's right?'

Sam swallowed. 'You mean —'

Sammie nodded grimly. 'Not being funny,' she said, 'but you are a bit . . . sidckickular. Slightly. Ish.'

'Not being funny,' he said, 'but you are a bit . . . un-nice. Maybe. A lot.'

That was the thing about being a twin. You couldn't have any secrets, at all.

9

SECRET #3:

SAM PAGET-SKIDELSKY IS A TOTAL MUPPET

On Saturday night they had early dinner so Mum Gen and Mum K could go out with Pea's mum.

The Llewellyn family lived next door: Clover, Pea and Tinkerbell, one mum, and a dog called Wuffly.

Clover – bit weird

Pea – nice; not a vegetable

Tinkerbell – approach with caution

Wuffly

Bree – not cheese-like

The mum was called Bree, which Sam thought was a shame, as she had nice yellow hair and was not at all cheese-like. She wrote glittery books about mermaids under the name Marina Cove, which was better, but Sam preferred to think of her as 'Pea's mum'.

Clover was like a smaller teenage version of Pea's mum, only louder. At weekends she liked to borrow the piano in their study to 'practise her self-expression' by singing all of *Frozen*, twice.

Tinkerbell – who was eight, yet fearsome – was as fond of burned things, explosions and danger as Sammie. At present, however, she seemed to be especially fond of staying dry – judging by the wellies, plastic mac and yellow plastic rain hat she was wearing on top of a bright blue wetsuit.

Pea, the middle sister, was Sam's best friend. She was older than him – and also a girl, as Halid had once pointed out in alarm when he'd come round for tea and found her in the kitchen, wearing a skirt and everything – but he liked her anyway. She was Co-Writer of *The Continuing Adventures of Captain Samazing*, in charge of plot twists and hard spelling.

'We *so* don't need Clover to babysit,' said Sammie as Mum K fluffed up her blue hair in the long hall mirror. 'We're totally old and responsible.'

'Of course you are,' said Pea's mum, stroking Surprise's nose. 'Positively elderly. But Clover wanted to borrow your piano anyway – didn't you, flower?'

Clover nodded her blonde head. 'I've got an audition piece to practise for Theatre Camp. You can be my audience, if you like?'

'I'd rather be disembowelled,' said Tinkerbell lightly. 'Besides, I've got atmospheric pressure to build.'

She produced a heavy carved wooden object from her mac pocket, with two glass-covered dials set into it, like an odd clock. She tapped the glass, and wrinkled her nose critically.

'Tink's decided to achieve godlike control of the weather,' explained Pea, to Mum Gen and Mum K's blank faces. 'She's trying to make it rain.'

They all turned to the open front door and peered out at the bright blue sky. It was mid-June, and London was in the grip of a glorious summer heatwave.

'It's not really working so far,' Pea added.

'But why?' asked Mum K.

'To fill up the swimming pool in our back garden,' said Tinkerbell, lifting the dials over her head and tapping the glass again.

'What swimming pool?'

'Duh. We haven't dug it yet,' said Sammie, rolling her eyes. Come on, Tink.'

They hurried upstairs, Surprise at Sammie's heels.

'Well, we appreciate you being here anyway,' said Mum Gen, giving Clover's arm a squeeze. 'Be stern! And you've got my number, yes? Call the moment anything makes a smashing noise.'

'Preferably before!' added Pea's mum as they slammed the front door behind them.

Sam and Pea fled upstairs, before Clover could insist they perform an interpretive dance to her piano plinking.

The attic ladder was down again, and the green landing carpet was covered in more of Mum K's dusty cardboard boxes.

'It's loads bigger than your room, Pea!' shouted Tinkerbell, her yellow plastic hat poking out of the trapdoor.

The Llewellyns' house was a mirror image of the Paget-Skidelskys', on the other side of the wall. Pea's bedroom was in the attic; a tiny white-painted room, with its own little wooden staircase and a sloping ceiling.

Pea clanked cheerfully up the ladder to see. 'Coming, Sam?'

She saw him hesitate.

Her face softened kindly; her head tilted sympathetically.

She *knew*. At once, as if it was not a surprise or a shock. As if she was a mum, not his friend.

Sam shook himself and took a deep breath. He wasn't a sidekick. He imagined Captain Samazing's cape around his shoulders, all billowy and impractical; pictured his arms going extra bulgy-muscled like Rohan's dad. He pictured Pointy at his heel, ready to clatter up after him into the *Pocket Rocket* cockpit.

He gripped the ladder.

From below, Clover's wobbly singing floated up like the soundtrack to his triumphant first ascent.

Sam climbed up in a very bold and assertive fashion – *one two three four*.

'See? You can do it!' said Pea encouragingly.

'He really can't,' said Sammie.

Sure enough, somewhere between rungs four and five, that slithering slug of terror slipped down his back and left him trembling.

'Are you all right, Sam?' asked Pea. 'You've gone all green and sweaty.'

'Like an avocado,' added Tinkerbell helpfully.

With his eyes shut, Sam staggered back down and lay flat on the green carpet among the dusty boxes.

Above, he could hear them quietly talking: about him, and about how Mum K's book really truly needed to be set on fire.

Pea would understand. Her mum had put all three Llewellyns in her *Mermaid Girl* books – and Pea's character had ended up evil and dead by book three. At least Mum K wasn't going to give him a fishtail and kill him in hers.

Her head appeared through the hatch, sending him another uncomfortably kind look. Then she clanked down the ladder and tiptoed downstairs as Clover's warbly voice went on swirling up through the floor. When she came back, she had a little plate with four malted milk biscuits – the ones with pictures of cows on.

'Here. Carbohydrates are a natural tranquillizer – we did it at school.'

Sam sat up and took a biscuit, biting around the bigger cow.

He did feel more tranquil.

'It doesn't matter,' said Pea reassuringly. 'How often do you need to go up ladders anyway?'

Sam groaned, and pressed the rest of the biscuit into his mouth all at once to push the groan back in.

'Ha!' said Tinkerbell, adjusting her rain hat. She explained all about Treetops: the galloping on horses, the rope bridges and the DEATH SLIDE OF DOOM (for which she put on a deep, booming voice, followed by authentic screaming). 'Mr Vine told us all about it. It's all jumping off stuff and climbing over things, and you even choose your own bedtime. I can't wait to be in Class Six. Mr Vine said one year someone broke their leg and got to go in a helicopter, with the leg in a box next to them because it fell off. Mr Vine didn't tell me that bit, but Jade Johnson's sister said it's definitely true.'

'It does sound more of a Sammie thing than a

Sam one,' said Pea eventually, studying each of them in turn. 'I mean, not that you aren't brave, Sam. But more in an indoors sort of way.'

Sam groaned again.

It was no good. He was Sam B. He was a side-kick, and he hadn't even noticed.

'It's all right for you,' said Sammie miserably, clomping down the ladder and perching on rung number three. 'You've only got to do the DEATH SLIDE OF DOOM for about thirty seconds – less, if you fall off. But at least you'll have people to scoop up your squashed and broken limbs afterwards. I looked in Miss Townie's desk at all the Treetops Homework Quizzes, and no one put me down as their friend. Not even Reema.'

'You did stab her in the leg with a propelling pencil last week,' said Sam quietly. 'And . . . other things.'

'I was just trying to get her attention!'

'Um,' said Sam. 'Maybe if you want to be best friends with someone, you could try not stabbing them with a pencil?'

'Can I stab Emily with a pencil instead? She might get lead poisoning and have to go to hospital

and be too ill to come to Treetops after all . . .'
Sammie brightened for a moment.

Suddenly there was a massive thump as a thick book dropped through the trapdoor and landed slap on the carpet in a puff of dust.

'Whoops,' called Tinkerbell innocently from above.

'Tink!' yelled Pea. 'That nearly— Oh! *Oh.*'

The book was from Mum Gen's therapeutic collection: *Vanquish That Fear! Exposure therapies for the 10 most common phobias.* There was a long list of things to be afraid of written in smaller print on the cover – along with a photo of a huge hairy spider, which Sam thought was a bit thoughtless.

'No, that's the whole point,' said Pea, turning it over to read the back page. 'Exposure therapy. It means you have to put yourself closer to the thing you're afraid of – just a little bit more each time, until it stops being scary.'

'Like when Dr Skidelsky learned how to like Surprise?' said Tinkerbell, dangling her head out of the ceiling above them.

Mum K was still more of a dog-tolerater than a dog-lover, but she used to hide in the kitchen from next-door's Wuffly, and shudder at the merest thought of a licky tongue. Surprise had been a very effective cure.

'Exactly like that,' said Pea. She flipped through the pages. 'Look, *acrophobia* – an acute fear of heights. That's what you've got, Sam.'

'I haven't,' said Sam.

Acrophobia didn't sound like the kind of thing a superhero was allowed to have. No one would ever send for Captain Acrophobia to rescue their children from Terrible Kidnappers or invading squids.

But then he read the list of symptoms – sweaty palms, shortness of breath, dizzy sensations, an irrational fear of falling – and it sounded so exactly like the crawling slug that he had to eat another cow biscuit at once.

'This says you should look at photographs of tall buildings while doing Attentive Breathing. And you should repeat Validating Statements so you feel all strong and non-wobbly when you think about high places.'

I am a powerful eagle, soaring on an air current and enjoying the magnificent view.

I am a lily pad floating on the surface of a cool lake.

I am relaxed and confident about achieving this task.

'Look, it even says you could try climbing a ladder! One step at a time, it says. That's what we should do. One extra step – one extra *rung* – every day. That's' – Pea looked up, counting – 'ten rungs altogether, plus one last step at the top. And you've done four already. How long until you go to Treetops?'

'Two weeks – ish.'

'Bags of time!' said Pea. 'We'll get you up into

that attic. We'll even have time to teach you how to come back down again!'

Sam looked up at Tinkerbell's head, hanging upside down out of the ceiling high above, and imagined himself up there at the top too, like Captain Samazing and Pointy in the cockpit of the *Pocket Rocket*, ready to be heroes.

He could do it.

He would do it.

He wasn't just a sidekick.

He was a powerful eagle.

He was a lily pad.

He was Captain Samazing, and he was going to get up that ladder.

10

VANQUISH
THAT FEAR!

Phobia checklist:
- Do you become nauseous even thinking about Emily?
- Does being in the presence of Emily make your heartbeat unusually rapid?
- Would removing these feelings about Emily completely change your life?
- If the answer is yes, it sounds like you have a case of Emilyphobia!
- But don't despair! Start the Vanquish That Fear! ten-week aversion therapy programme today!

'You can't have Emilyphobia,' said Sam as they walked into Class Six on Monday morning. 'That is, like, not even a thing.'

Sammie shook her head. 'The book only lists the ten most *common* phobias, for boring people like you. Mine's all unusual and exotic. But I've definitely got one.'

Sammie had read the symptoms for *arachnophobia* – an acute fear of spiders – and they were all remarkably familiar.

Instead of scuttly legs making her queasy, it was pale pink spectacles.

When Emily and Reema's hairclips bumped together – puppies today, not cherries, matching puppies; who even made hairclips with puppies on? – it sent her cold, just like spotting a big creepy-crawlie dart under the sofa.

And the mere sight of that grey wool cardigan, with its six pearly buttons neatly fastened, was exactly like a tarantula walking over her skin.

It was reassuring, in a way. It wasn't her fault she wasn't friends with Reema any more. She had a medical condition.

Also she liked imagining Emily's head with six

spidery legs growing out of it – and her own left trainer squashing it flat.

'Anyway, you're just jealous because I'm going to win at aversion therapy,' she said to Sam. 'Bet I vanquish my fear quicker than you.'

Unfortunately, Emilyphobia proved hard to shift.

Sammie slotted a friendly note into Emily's pencil case –

You are my very favourite Natterjack Toad.

– but Emily frowned at it and threw it away.

Sammie stole her socks after PE (what better compliment to someone's taste in socks could there be? Even though they were weird frilled ones like napkins in a posh restaurant) – but Emily told Miss Townie.

She even, nobly, left half her lunch-time Kit-Kat in the hated cardigan pocket as a surprise – but Emily left it on the sunniest windowsill to go melty.

'Go away!' shouted Reema, helping Emily scrub the chocolate off the inside of her pocket. 'Just leave us alone!' And she slammed the toilet door in

Sammie's face, and leaned against it so she couldn't get in.

It was a bit awful.

Half a Kit-Kat, wasted. Which was a whole one, really, because they didn't sell half ones in shops.

By the end of the week it was time to get serious.

Dear Emily,

I am sorry about the Kit-Kat in your cardigan. This was wrong because I wanted you to eat it, not melt it all over your clothing. In future I will insert all chocolaty gifts directly into your face.

I think we could be friends if we just spent more time in close proximity under supervision.

Come to my house on Saturday at 10 a.m. for FUN TIMES and LAUGHTER and playing with my dog etc. You are new and it's important to have more than one friend because you never know when she might suddenly turn evil and ignore you. Also you can't say no because I already told my mums.

From Sammie

Sammie had not, in fact, told her mums, so when Emily and her dad appeared on the doorstep on Saturday morning, Mum Gen was still in her nightie.

'Morning,' said Emily's dad warily as a loud thud echoed from upstairs: Mum K, dropping more cobwebbed boxes down the attic ladder. 'Just wondering what time I should pick her up?'

'Sorry?' said Mum Gen, yawning as she knotted her dressing gown. 'I don't see clients on the weekends, I'm afraid, but—'

'Mu-um,' said Sammie crossly, hurling herself forward and firmly pushing Mum Gen's spotty slippers out of sight behind the front door. 'This is my friend Emily. She's come over to do friend stuff. You can pick her up at three o'clock. Bye!'

With a barely repressed shudder of revulsion, she gripped Emily's wrist and hauled her into the house. Five hours seemed a revoltingly long time to have to spend with a human spider, but she'd added up all the *two minutes looking at a spider video on YouTube* and *five minutes visualization of a spider in your hair* and reckoned she might as well get them all over with in one go.

Another enormous thud came from upstairs.

'You can phone me if you'd like to come home

early!' called Emily's dad from the doorstep in a worried voice. Then he was gone.

Emily stood in the kitchen, blinking.

Sammie eyed her with suspicion. Emily was wearing skinny jeans, strappy sandals, and a pale lemon top that slipped off one shoulder (no bra; Sammie felt itchy under her strawberry print), and her swishy hair hung loose down her back, free of all fruit and/or animal accompaniments.

Simply disgusting.

Meanwhile Sammie had topped off her usual jeans and football shirt with a cardigan, to demonstrate her willingness to compromise/general nicery. (Alas, the only one she could find was a fluffy red Christmas one of Mum Gen's, with pine-tree pockets and buttons shaped like puddings, which smelled of dog and mouldy oranges. But one had to suffer for friendship.)

'Thank you for inviting me over,' said Emily stiffly, her voice soft and whispery even though she wasn't hiding behind her hand; a hideous-creature sort of voice, exactly like something that lived in the dark and spun webs and might be poisonous. 'My dad says it's very nice of you.'

'It is,' said Sammie, nodding. 'I am nice.'

And she gripped Emily's arm again (*In these initial periods of exposure, slowly build your tolerance from two seconds to ten*) and pulled her into the garden.

They played football ('Reema loves football – you'd better learn how if you're going to stay being her friend,' Sammie said helpfully), but Emily bruised her bare toes. They sat together on the top of the monkey bars ('Reema likes the view from up here – you can see into other people's houses and make up names for them, like Dave No-Curtains and Bendy Pilates Lady – she can fold herself up like an envelope'), but the lemon top got rust on it. Then Emily asked, 'What's that?' in her spider-voice, pointing at the pillow dangling from the shed door with a twig javelin embedded in one hand-drawn nostril – and Sammie decided that was enough of the garden.

'Is it working?' asked Sam while she made blackcurrant squash for them both in the kitchen.

Sammie shrugged. 'I feel very sick, but I don't think I'll actually *be* sick, you know? I don't know how to fill up five hours of continuous Emily-exposure, though. What do girls like doing?'

Sam put his head on one side. 'Reading books. Though that might just be Pea. Um. Shopping?'

Sammie took Emily to Tesco. They bought a bag of onions.

Then they came back.

'That was weird,' hissed Emily.

'Reema really likes onions,' said Sammie encouragingly, and took the opportunity to sniff Emily's hair.

Lunch was no better: a chicken pie that Mum K had made the night before, which would've been perfect for four but stretched round five meagrely. When Mum Gen lifted the dish and said, 'Who wants this last slice?' – everyone said yes, and it had to be chopped into individual mouthfuls.

Emily picked at her pudding, staring from one end of the table to the other.

'Not being rude, but,' she said eventually, in her shiver-inducing whisper, close in Sammie's ear, 'where's your dad?'

Mum Gen and Mum K exchanged looks as Sammie felt her face heat up.

'We don't have one,' said Sam. 'Everyone knows that.'

It wasn't strictly true; they had a donor dad called Malcolm, who had a moustache, and occasionally sent a polite letter to encourage them to maintain good oral hygiene and eat more oats. But he wasn't a *dad* sort of dad. The Paget-Skidelskys were two mums, two Sams and a dog. That was how it was. That was how she wanted it to stay, for ever and ever.

'But,' whispered Emily again, tilting her spoon towards Mum Gen, 'if that's your mum . . . who's that?' She was looking at Mum K now.

'Also their mum,' said Mum K dryly. 'Mind-blowing, isn't it?'

Emily put down her spoon, as if it truly was.

'Reema knows all about it,' Sammie said quickly. 'Reema used to come over all the time, without minding.'

And it was true, but Sammie could feel Mum Gen's eyes on her cheek, and felt hot and embarrassed and quite angry at all the spiders in the world, for ever.

After lunch Sammie and Emily sat on the squashy bean-bags to watch TV, Sammie reluctantly edging hers millimetre by millimetre across the kitchen floor until their elbows touched.

'Why are you counting?' whispered Emily, shuffling away.

'No reason,' said Sammie, shuffling closer with a grimace. *Sixteen, seventeen* . . .

'Why is your dog green?' asked Emily, sliding onto the floor.

'No reason,' said Sammie, slipping down after her.

Surprise padded over, tail perked and curious, and curled up on Emily's lap. Then he did an enormous dribble, and when he padded away, there was a fresh puppy tooth resting on Emily's knee.

Emily screamed.

That was the end of Emily exposure therapy. Her dad was called, and Mum Gen stood on the doorstep with them both, apologizing profusely as they drove away.

Sammie was summoned back to the kitchen table for A Talk.

'It's lovely that you've made a new friend,' said Mum Gen, in her maximum Professionally Gentle voice. 'But you do have to tell us if you've invited someone to the house, so we don't accidentally starve them. And she was obviously a bit surprised to find two mums.'

'So?' said Sammie. 'It's like those people being mean to us in a park. Their problem, not mine.'

Mum K quirked one eyebrow above her glasses. 'She has a point.'

Mum Gen frowned. 'In a perfect world, perhaps. But let's be practical here. You might like to mention us beforehand, and give her a chance to ask any questions she might have. That way, she won't be put on the spot. You'd like to invite her over again after all, hmm?'

'Urgh,' said Sammie. 'No way! Anyway, I don't need to. I am completely cured.'

And she strolled out into the garden, and hung the pillowcase target back up on the shed door. She looked into the pale pink-spectacled face and smiled. She felt nothing: no shivers, no shakes.

But she gave the other nostril a quick javelin, just to make sure.

11

SECRET #4:

SAM PAGET-SKIDELSKY IS A
SOAP BUBBLE ON A GENTLE BREEZE

Sam, meanwhile, had been making slow progress Vanquishing His Fear.

On Monday he had made it up to rung number six, muttering, 'Light as a down feather floating up through a cloud,' under his breath.

On Tuesday he had been an aerobatic swift, soaring high to rung number seven.

On Wednesday and Thursday he had been too full of hummus to be a dust mote in a shaft of light, so he concentrated on drawing heroics instead. (It was taking quite a long time to go through all the

Captain Samazings, rubbing out his arms and adding extra-bulgy muscles like Mr Grover's.)

On Friday he had asked Paolo if he could borrow his spray-on deodorant after PE.

'Eww,' said Sammie, wrinkling up her nose. 'You smell old.'

'The word you're looking for is *manly*,' said Sam. 'I smell *manly*. It says on the tin.'

When he got home, his mums did not think he smelled manly. They thought he smelled hilarious. And it still didn't get him up past rung number seven.

Saturday had been spent entirely avocado-faced, as Sam tried, and tried, and tried again to be a confident eagle all the way up to rung number eight, to no avail – and on Sunday morning he didn't get the chance to even begin.

'Is this entirely necessary at seven o'clock on a Sunday?' asked Mum Gen blearily, peeking out of their bedroom in her pyjamas as Mum K clanked up and down the ladder.

'Yes!' yelled Mum K, shooing Surprise out of her path with a not-so-gentle nudge of her trainer. 'I want to live in a house where I can open a door without falling over ten boxes of crap.'

'Our children's treasured possessions, you mean?' called Mum Gen.

'Are you throwing away Whirry Bunny?' shouted Sammie from her bed.

'Or important artworks that should be saved for posterity?' Sam called.

'Probably!' said Mum K, cheerfully hurling a bin bag down the stairs.

The morning was spent in subterfuge.

Mum K would carry a box down to the front door.

Under instructions to deliver it to the Bad House skip, Sam or Sammie would collect it, then carry it instead round the front of the house, leaning over the prickly rose bush to return it to Mum Gen, sitting inside in her dressing gown, to rifle through and check it for Treasuredness.

While Mum K was working through all the boxes in the study, Mum Gen hid things behind the golden sofas. Sam carried the rescued things back up the stairs, and Sammie took them up the ladder.

Then, while Mum Gen was at church, Mum K aggressively vacuumed and dusted and Lemon Zing-squirted the entire house, before anyone was even allowed to think about what to do for Sammie's Family Day Out.

The ladder was tucked away, and the trapdoor clicked shut in the ceiling.

'And don't you dare go mucking about with it,' said Mum K sharply. 'Not now this place actually looks faintly like my – *our* – house again.'

'Charming!' said Mum Gen. 'As if a little clutter ever hurt anyone . . .'

There was only one more week until Treetops, and the DEATH SLIDE OF DOOM.

Sam was running out of time. Suddenly he was plunged into a mysterious world where failure was a real, sincere possibility.

'Don't stress,' said Sammie blithely. 'I've got this aversion-therapy thing nailed. You leave it to me.'

Sam was not convinced. He felt even less so when Sammie's plans for her Family Day Out were whispered into his mums' ears at lunch time, accompanied by a vaguely sinister smug grin.

'Oh yes!' said Mum Gen, clapping her hands. 'Great idea!'

'Can't believe we've never done it before,' said Mum K.

That meant it couldn't be the zoo, or swimming, or the cinema – and not endless family football where he always had to be goalie. But Sammie looked *extremely* pleased with herself.

The journey took more than half an hour. They got off the tube at North Greenwich, far down on the south-east side of London – right by the river, according to the map. In fact, after a few minutes' walk, Sam could see the white curve and yellow spikes of the Millennium Dome.

THE AIRLINE, said a sign, with an arrow.

'Are we going on a *plane*?' asked Sam.

But Sammie shook her head, pushed him forward and pointed up with a grin.

Hanging impossibly high in the cloudless blue sky was a row of red cable cars, slowly moving up a steep swinging cable and then travelling in a series of dips and rises, back and forth across the Thames.

'Perfect day for it!' said Mum Gen.

'I've been wanting to do this for ages,' said Mum K.

'Oh,' said Sam as a familiar cold slug-like sensation slid down his neck.

'Come on,' said Sammie, dragging him towards the turnstiles.

Unlike getting on a real plane, there was no long security check, no hours of waiting. They went up an escalator and down some stairs and that was it.

Boarding.

The red cable cars didn't stop to let you on; they moved slowly along in a semicircle, doors open, ready for you to hop in before they took off, and up, and up. Ahead, you could see the thin black cable swinging out into the open air, and the cars ahead looping up and down – with more returning from the other side.

A woman in a hi-vis jacket smiled, and waved them towards the next empty car.

Mum K leaped in, laughing. Sammie followed. Mum Gen frowned and had to walk alongside the car for a few paces to catch up with it before hopping aboard.

'Hurry up!' called Sammie, frantically beckoning.

'Just step across. It's easy, I promise,' said Mum Gen.

Sam sidestepped, and sidestepped, keeping pace with the open door – but he was running out of semicircle.

'Sam – if you don't . . .'

'You have to . . .'

'Take my hand . . .'

'Doors closing,' said the woman in the hi-vis jacket, rather urgently.

'Oh Lord,' said Mum Gen, and she scooped up her long skirts and hopped back out at the very last moment.

The cable car jerked forward, its doors sliding shut. Then it swooped out into the open, with Mum K and Sammie's faces pressed against the glass, mouths open, horrified but laughing.

'No fear, mate, happens all the time,' said the woman in the hi-vis jacket, throwing Sam a conspiratorial wink. 'Hop in the next one? You'll be able to wave across at your friends, then.'

The next cable car was already halfway round the semicircle. Sam sidestepped along next to it. But it slid past, and out, and up up up.

'I could hold your hand,' said Mum Gen. 'Or – would you like to step on first?'

A small queue was beginning to form behind them.

Another empty car went by.

The hi-vis lady beckoned a few families forward. They slipped in front, all apologies. Mum Gen smiled, waving them through, then steered Sam over to a corner.

'Sam.' She knelt down and looked him in the eye. 'Would you rather not go on the cable car today?'

Sam looked at the swinging loops of cable, and the river far, far below, and thought that he would rather not go on the cable cars ever at all in his whole entire life. But instead he just nodded.

Mum Gen took him to Starbucks for a calming smoothie while they waited for Mum K and Sammie to come back across.

'What a shame,' she said. 'Sammie was so sure you'd love it! She said you'd been wishing you'd picked it yourself last week.'

Sammie was, apparently, just as confident that Sam would love the view from Tower Bridge (the top struts had lifts going up – Sam decided not to bother) and the top of the Monument (311 steps up a spiral staircase inside a giant column – Sam got as far as step 77 before the curving stone walls suddenly seemed to press in on him, and the view of outside through the tiny windows began to tilt, and Mum K had to walk him all the way back down, stepping carefully in front, with Sam's hands on her shoulders so as to be sure of not tripping).

At the bottom, a man handed them each a certificate.

This is to certify that

. . . .

has walked all 311 steps to the top of the Monument

'Nope,' said Mum K, and passed the certificates back.

Sam sat slumped and silent as the tube took them home across London. He had never felt more side-kickular in his life.

'Sorry,' whispered Sammie when they got home – but he shuffled away from her.

'Sorry,' she said again, outside his shut bedroom door.

Sorry, said the note she pushed underneath it, along with a crumply clump of paper: a pile of Mum Gen's old letters and printed-out emails.

Dear Kara,

Disaster! Sam's lost Taggy. I know, I know, you think five's too old to have a Taggy – he shouldn't be dependent on an emotional connection with an inanimate bit of fabric, etc., etc. – but you're not the one listening to him sob his heart out while ransacking every room in the house.

Correction! Taggy is still lost – but disaster averted. Get this: Sam found her old Taggy, snipped it in half with the kitchen scissors (I know, I am the Worst Mum, I'll put them somewhere higher up) and gave him half. Both now snuggled up and sleeping peacefully.

Hi K,
Just a quick one – do we really need to get them into separate bedrooms right now? Janey from PP Club said she was looking for child-size bunk-beds but just broached it

with the Sams and — universal horror! Well, from her anyway. Don't think he minded, but apparently she 'likes listening to him breathe so she knows he's not dead'.

Kara – can't wait for you to see this at the weekend! Sam won the school Design-a-Robot competition (it's called Cheesebot and makes sandwiches – you'll cry laughing when you see it). Was expecting epic sulky meltdown from her when she didn't get a prize, but instead she made him a medal. Out of CHEESE. Now they're sitting on the kitchen floor building a Cheesebot out of loo rolls.

Maybe you should write a book about twins, and how actually having two at once can be fantastic, for all those terrified parents out there?

Under the letter was a note.

Dear Sam,
Sorry I made you do too much aversion therapy. This was wrong because it didn't work — but I only did it because I'm nice and the Best Twin, see. In future I will

not make you go on high things that make you go avocado.

I could point out as well that I gave my whole Family Day to do a thing to help you, but am Too Nice to so I won't.

Sam sighed, and opened the door a crack. 'Maybe aversion therapy just doesn't work on me,' he said.

Sammie nodded unhelpfully – then saw his face. 'Oh! I mean – bet it does. That was probably too much all at once. I mean, I got cured of Emilyphobia really fast, but I've only had it for a few weeks. You've got years and years of being hopeless and pathetic to get over.'

And she patted the top of his head, not very comfortingly at all.

'Where's the dog?' asked Sam later, when they were all squashing onto the two bean-bag chairs in the kitchen to watch *Ponyo*.

'Happily, not dribbling anywhere near me,' said Mum K, sipping her coffee.

When the film was finished, they checked all over the house.

'He knows he's not allowed in there,' said Mum Gen as they pulled out golden sofa cushions in the front room. (Surprise had been known to leave surprises in people's shoes – the wet kind you wouldn't want to step in – and Mum Gen often told her unhappy people to take off their shoes. Apparently it is easier to cheer up with a nice fluffy carpet to squish between your toes.)

'The filthy beast will be under our bed again, eating something expensive,' said Mum K. 'And someone else can clean whatever he pukes up later.'

THINGS SURPRISE HAS EATEN:
- 14oz aged Parmesan cheese
- a purple sock ––> interesting woolly poo
- three tennis balls
- a lifetime supply of toilet rolls
- pages 243–312 of *Mindfulness: Think Yourself to Contentment* by Dr Emmeline Fish

Sam ate roast dinner. He lay on his stripy bedroom rug, drawing Pointy at the controls of the *Pocket Rocket* at the exact moment it was discovered that the SADS (Squid Alert Detection System) had reached Ominous Green for danger.

But when it was time for that week's new *Tiny Robot Unicorn Friends*, Surprise was still nowhere to be found.

Sam watched Cha-Cha and Minty get imprisoned by the Moon Wizard, which was about the most exciting beginning to an episode of *Tiny Robot Unicorn Friends* ever – but he was too worried to concentrate.

Surprise wasn't under the bed.

He wasn't in the back garden, digging up the patio, having left a helpful breadcrumb trail of fallen teeth.

He wasn't behind the piano, doing a naughty poo.

He wasn't in any of the kitchen cupboards, or bedroom drawers, or in the laundry basket under all the pyjama bottoms.

Surprise wasn't anywhere.

'He'll show up when he's hungry,' said Mum Gen, in a Professionally Gentle way. 'He'll be back by morning – you'll see.'

But he wasn't.

When Sam ran down the stairs on Monday morning to find him, there was no telltale patter of paws on the hall floor, no waggy tail saying hello – and his bowl (yellow, with *SURPRISE!* painted around the edge in Sam's own wobbly blue capitals) was still full of yesterday's Puppies' Crunchy Munch, quite untouched.

The dog was lost.

12

Dear Surprise,

I'm really, really sorry I dyed you green that time. It was only because I needed to walk past Reema in the park and if my dog was green then she would have to think, 'Wow, I wish I had a green dog — the girl with a green dog must be way better than Emily Roche,' and then she would be my friend again. But actually you were too sad to be taken to the park.

Anyway if that's why you ran away, I'm really, really sorry.

If it's because of there not being a Dog Tooth Fairy, I'm sorry about that too. When you come home I will give you a pound myself.

If it's because of Mum K being mean, I promise to javelin her in the ear repeatedly.

Please come home?

Love from Sammie

'Whatever it is, do I have to care about it before coffee?' moaned Mum K as Sammie and Sam dragged her down the stairs with her blue-streaked hair on end.

'The dog,' said Mum Gen, sternly pointing at the uneaten bowl of food (*For Healthy Bones and Happy Pups!*) 'is *missing*.'

'Did you leave the back door open yesterday?' demanded Sammie.

It was bound to be that. Not her and the green dye. Bound to be.

'Everyone knows you're not allowed to leave the back door open,' said Sam darkly. '*Everyone*.'

'Why are you all blaming me?' asked Mum K.

'Because he's never gone missing before, not ever! Not till you came home.' Sammie suddenly felt sick with worry. 'And . . . you aren't nice to him.'

'I'm perfectly nice to that ridiculous bloody dog!'

'Not sure that's helping your case, Kara dear,' said Mum Gen, spotting Sammie's fists clenching, and steering both twins back upstairs to get dressed. 'Don't panic. He'll be in the house somewhere. Though perhaps if Mum K happens to remember that she might have left the back door ever so slightly open . . .'

There was a lot of door-slamming downstairs while Sammie got dressed in jeans and T-shirt, and some shouting too. That had never happened until Mum K came home, either.

'Where's your school uniform?' said Mum Gen when Sammie hurried back down to put on her trainers.

'We can't go to school! We have to find Surprise.'

Mum K rolled her eyes as Sam appeared wearing jeans too. 'Pffrt! I don't think so. Breakfast – then go and change. He'll turn up. He's only a dog.'

'He's not *only* a dog,' mumbled Sam, horrified.

'He's *our* dog,' said Sammie.

Their own dribbly, gap-toothed, moss-green dog. OK, so one time she'd tried to ride him round the park and his legs had gone bandy. True, she sometimes shut the door on him at night, because he did farts that smelled like meat pie with mushrooms. And if there had been a Dog Tooth Fairy, she might have borrowed his pound. But she did love him. She loved him just as much as Sam did, and Sam looked like he might be about to cry.

'Should we call the police?' she asked, her eyes wide and worried.

Mum Gen shook her head; you only did that for missing people, apparently. But while Sammie and Sam picked miserably at muesli and apple juice, she phoned all the vets and the animal sanctuary, in case someone had left a Surprise on their doorstep.

They had not.

'No news is good news,' said Mum Gen, though she didn't sound at all sure. 'And Mum K's quite right: you can't miss school. You'll only sit here and worry.'

For Sam, it turned out that sitting at home worrying might have been a better plan.

He had forgotten his reading diary, his water bottle and his trainers for PE – and on any normal school day Miss Townie would've frowned, and then knelt down and asked what was wrong – and when he explained, she would've been kind and perhaps let him sit in the Reading Nook instead of doing indoor gym and bean-bag-catching, so he could be quiet and sad by himself.

But when they got to school, there was no smiling Miss Townie at the front of the class. It was Mrs McMin.

'At great personal inconvenience,' she announced, 'I shall be taking Class Six today. Miss Townie is unwell.'

A shiver went through the room.

'Is it the baby?' asked Sam, looking at the little dinosaur pinned to the News Board. 'Is that why she's poorly?'

Mrs McMin looked at Sam in vague recognition. She checked his name against the register and curled her upper lip. 'You will put your hand up in my classroom if you wish to ask a question.'

Sam put his hand up, but Mrs McMin ignored it, and sent Nishat scuttling around with a pile of maths books as if there was a whole swarm of bees behind her.

She ignored it again when Sam tried to explain why he couldn't fill in his reading diary.

'Miss, it's not his fault, our dog's lost,' protested Sammie when Sam was asked to tell the whole class why everyone else had written a paragraph about the sky god Itzamna and he had merely drawn a picture of a sad cloud.

'If this is how much you pay attention at home, I'm not at all surprised,' said Mrs McMin, looming over him.

'I didn't lose him,' murmured Sam. 'It's not my fault.'

'It's really not, Sam,' whispered Halid.

'Course not,' said Honey.

But Mrs McMin rapped a ruler on the table to stop any talking, and made Sam sit at her desk all through break to catch up. Sam found it impossible to care about the sky god Itzamna under the circumstances, so he had to sit there through lunch too.

For the first time ever Mum K was exactly on time to collect them at the end of the day – but the guilty slope of her shoulders spoke volumes.

'Before you ask, I've called the vets again,' she said quickly, 'and the animal sanctuary. There's just no sign of Surprise anywhere.'

They walked the long way home, through the park, just in case. Suddenly there were dogs everywhere: happy dogs, bouncy dogs, barky ones and tiny ones that yipped and needed to be carried

up steps – and all their happy, bouncy owners, smiling as they threw chewy bones or called out for 'Possum!' or 'Spot! Spotty! Spotty dog!' to come.

At home, Surprise's favourite orange chewy carrot sat on the front doorstep as a lure – still unclaimed.

'Next door might know something . . .' suggested Sammie.

They knocked on the Llewellyns' raspberry-red front door – but Pea's mum hadn't seen Surprise either.

'And I'd definitely have noticed. Wuffly would've too, wouldn't you, girl?' she said, ruffling Wuffly's hairy ears fondly as the dog jumped up. 'Because Surprise so licky and barky and full of beans.'

'That's one way to put it,' muttered Mum K.

'You aren't allowed to talk about him,' said Sammie. 'It's your fault he's gone!'

'I did not leave the back door open!'

'Then why is he missing?'

There was an awkward silence.

Pea's mum gently suggested that Mum K might like to get on with some work at home, and then she gave them biscuits – a natural tranquillizer, Sam remembered, and took two, for his nerves – and let them search the garden for clues (dug-up flowers, chewed valuables) until Clover and Pea got home. Tinkerbell arrived soon after, from after-school club.

They were all horrified to hear the news.

'Oh no,' said Pea. 'For a whole night and all today? Have you looked inside the washing machine?'

'We've looked *everywhere*,' said Sam.

'Everywhere inside your house . . .' said Tinkerbell slowly. 'If he's run away – or someone's taken him home by mistake – then he could be in someone else's washing machine! Or— Ooh, maybe he's been kidnapped!'

'He's a dog, not a kid,' snapped Sammie.

'Dognapped, then!' Tinkerbell seemed worryingly thrilled by the idea.

Clover, meanwhile, looked pained. 'Or he could have been hit by a car. Sorry, but . . . Wuffly did get knocked down once, right outside our house.'

It was a horrible thought. Sam knelt down and stroked Wuffly's crooked back leg, where it had mended. Wuffly licked his biscuity hand and nuzzled his neck, as if she understood why he was sad – but the licky feeling just made him miss Surprise even more.

Captain Samazing was nothing without his co-pilot Pointy.

Surprise-less Sam was too awful to contemplate.

'Search party,' said Pea firmly. 'That's what we need: teams looking for him, so we can cover more ground. Clover, you stay here in case he's found while we're out. Mum, Tink and Sammie can take Queen's Park and all the streets on the way. Sam, me and you can check all the front gardens on this street, all the way up to the shops. We'll take Wuffly too. She might sniff him out.'

Sam and Sammie exchanged nods. Sam felt better at once, now he was *doing* something.

Pea fetched a furled yellow umbrella with a pointy end, for prodding bushes. Tinkerbell put her wetsuit on over her clothes ('Just in case,' she said, tapping the barometer ominously before putting it in her pocket). Sammie nipped next door, and returned with a broom-handle javelin for bush-prodding, and the toy carrot from their doorstep, so Wuffly would have something Surprise-y to sniff.

They set off in opposite directions, Wuffly tugging on her lead and snuffling the pavement at once.

Sam and Pea walked all along one side of their road, peering over bushes and cautiously poking the long umbrella underneath parked cars. Then they crossed over, and did the same on the other side. Wuffly sniffed and snuffled, leaping ahead to paw at one of Surprise's favourite weeing-on trees and lampposts and making Sam's heart leap with hope – but it was always some other dog she could smell.

Until they got to the Bad House.

Where Wuffly began to bark, and bark, and bark.

13

SECRET #5:

THERE'S SOMETHING IN THE BAD HOUSE

'What is it, Wuffs?' said Sam, dropping down and pressing his ear flat against Wuffly's hairy head as she strained at her lead. 'What can you smell, girl? Dognappers?'

As a cloud rolled across the blue sky and blocked the sun, the Bad House loomed up behind the rows of scaffolding. Between the gaps he could see blank dark windows, staring grimly back.

The Heavenly Construction van had gone, but the yellow skip was still on the mossy drive, now with a mouldy furled carpet hanging out of it, broken roof tiles – and a mountain of cardboard boxes, labelled *SAMS AGED 6–8* and *NOTES: CHILD DEVELOPMENT*.

Sam gasped. 'The boxes! Mum K took them out yesterday!'

'You don't think . . . ?' said Pea.

Sam threw aside the umbrella and, ignoring the smell and the thoughts of dead rotting bodies in rolled-up carpets, leaped into the skip and began pulling boxes open. He could picture it at once: the nosy puppy climbing into a box to find something to chew, and being carried outside and dropped into a skip as if he was rubbish . . . Any moment now, Sam would pull back a cardboard flap and find a wet black nose and a dopey, gappy, doggy smile greeting him, heroic, rescuing Samazing Sam with his cape billowing out behind his shoulders . . .

But Surprise's nose never appeared. The boxes were just full of papers, old notebooks and a few plastic toys. Sam emptied all the papers out, just in case – grazing his hand painfully on a piece of broken brick – but eventually he climbed out, rather more slowly than he'd climbed in.

'He's not there,' he said breathlessly. 'I can't find him.'

A breeze rippled through the overgrown brambles, and Wuffly began to bark again, just as urgently as before.

With a chill, Sam realized where he was standing: on the driveway of the Bad House, mere steps away from the front door.

Pea was still on the pavement, keeping well back and hanging onto Wuffly's collar for dear life, one wary eye on the grim old house.

'Here, Wuffs,' whispered Sam, holding the carrot under her nose again. 'Is that what you can smell? Is it Surprise? Is he . . . inside?'

Wuffly sniffed at the toy, but she didn't seem interested. Her ears went back, and she strained forward, barking, snarling, baring her teeth.

'I think she can smell something else,' said Sam, grabbing Wuffly's collar too to stop her from breaking loose. 'Something *bad*.'

'But it's empty,' said Pea, staring up at the blank windows. 'It's just an old empty house.'

The breeze lifted, rustling the bushes and whistling through the scaffolding – but behind it Sam thought he could hear the faint high sound of someone crying. Not a dog; not his Surprise, but someone small, and very helpless.

Wuffly barked and pulled even harder.

'Can you hear that?' whispered Sam, grabbing Pea's arm.

'Hear what?' she whispered back.

Then the wind dropped.

The clouds parted.

Sam closed his eyes, trying to catch the sound again – but it was gone, vanished with all the whistles and creaks of the scaffolding, and Wuffly was already tugging Pea off down the pavement, following a new scent.

He must've imagined it. No one could be living inside the Bad House.

He chased after Wuffly, and they checked the rest of their street and three others – but all Wuffly sniffed out were squirrels and old bits of poo from other dogs.

They trooped dejectedly back to Pea's house.

The other half of the search party was just as glum.

'No luck, I'm afraid,' said Pea's mum gently. 'And please apologize to your mums for the state of Sammie's trousers. I did tell her not to climb into that wheelie bin.'

'There's no point searching if you don't search

everywhere,' growled Sammie, peeling a slimy piece of potato peel off her elbow.

But now they had – and the dog was still lost.

'Posters,' said Pea firmly, 'for putting on lampposts and through letterboxes . . .' She hadn't given up hope. And she gave Sam another tranquillizing biscuit.

Sammie and Tinkerbell hurried next door to look for photographs of Surprise.

Pea and Sam went up to Pea's tiny attic bedroom at the very top of the house to plan their poster. Sam drew the big letters at the top and thought of the words, and Pea wrote them down so the spellings wouldn't confuse anyone.

LOST, DOG!

Identifying features: bouncy, dribbly, missing teeth. Likes carrots and chewing things. Answers to the following names:
Surprise, Puppy, Horrible Beast.
Lost on Sunday in Kensal Rise.
We miss him.
Please phone us up if you have seen him anywhere!

(Also look in your bins please.)

'Perfect,' said Pea.

Sam underlined *We miss him*, twice.

'Perfecter,' said Pea. 'Once Sammie comes back with the photo, we'll scan it on Mum's printer, and make a big pile of copies. We could put them up in school, and in the library, and . . .'

But Sam wasn't listening.

He could hear a noise: a whimpery, whiny crying.

He shook his head to clear out his ears. He was hearing things again, just like outside the Bad House.

But Pea was reaching over to clutch his wrist, her mouth falling open with a gasp. 'What's that?'

'You can hear it too?'

The whimpering grew louder. It was an awful sound; low, sad and very lonely – and apparently real enough for them both to hear it.

Sam peered under Pea's bed – but there was nothing there but dust and notebooks.

Pea shook her head. 'It's not coming from in here,' she whispered, edging towards the wall. She pressed her hands against it, then her ear, straining to hear.

Sam grabbed the little glass that sat on Pea's bedside table, threw the water out of the window, and held it up to the wall too, pressing one ear to the base like he'd seen in films.

To his surprise, it worked. A whimper echoed through the glass. It shivered through him, directly to his heart.

He took a step back, staring at the wall as he tried to think. 'The attic. Mum K put the ladder back up yesterday . . . and I didn't try to be a dust mote . . . We haven't looked—'

'I've got a photo!' called Sammie, from downstairs.

But Sam was already running, Pea close behind him, down two lots of stairs, past Sammie – who frowned and whirled and followed – and down the Llewellyns' crazy-paving path, swinging off the red-brick pillar between the houses to fling himself into their house, breathlessly, as fast as he could and still too slow.

'Hush! You know Mum Gen's working,' hissed Mum K, peeking out of the study as they thudded up the stairs. 'What are you doing?'

'No idea!' yelled Sammie.

'The pole – grab the pole,' said Pea as Sam reached up to hook the trapdoor open. His hands were shaking, and she had to help him hold it steady enough to find the catch, but eventually it clicked into place. The trapdoor swung open. The ladder slowly, silently unfurled itself.

From high above came a faint, feeble whine of misery. There was a pattering sound, and then a nose appeared, black and sniffly, peeping over the edge of the trapdoor.

'Surprise!' breathed Sammie.

And Sam climbed up the ladder – not even stopping to think about being a relaxed lily pad or a confident soap bubble – and leaped into the attic to wrap the lost, found puppy up in his arms.

14

SECRET #6:

SAM PAGET-SKIDELSKY IS SAMAZING
AFTER ALL AND NOT A BIT MUPPETY

'I can't believe we didn't hear him, poor thing,' said Mum Gen, who had temporarily abandoned her unhappy people to find out what all the fuss was about.

'I can't believe you shut him up here!' said Sammie, glaring at Mum K.

Surprise lay curled up in Sam's lap – not being squashed under a car or dognapped by Terrible Kidnappers after all, but here in the attic, safe and warm and a little bit smelly. Mum K's head poked up through the trapdoor as she balanced on the ladder and slid a water bowl under Surprise's nose – which he lapped at frantically.

'Neither can I,' said Mum K, wincing at the pong. (There were several small dried puddles on the wooden floorboards, along with an area which the puppy had apparently decided was Poo Corner and, underneath, a cleaner sort of chemical smell.) 'Didn't think he even knew how to climb ladders. Clever dog.'

She leaned in, and awkwardly stroked Surprise's ears. He nipped at her hand, and growled.

'And clever Sam, for working it out,' added Mum Gen quickly.

Sam smiled as Surprise quivered in his arms. There was a reproachful look in the puppy's big brown eyes, but his ears had begun to perk up again, and his tail wagged once or twice.

And that wasn't all.

Sam had made it up the ladder – quickly, thought-lessly, without his face going avocado-ish or the carpet going swimmy. He had a feeling he couldn't have done it without *needing* to – but still. He'd done it once. That meant he could do it again.

Sam was going to be just fine at Treetops.

He wasn't Sam B. He wasn't a sidekick. He was Captain Samazing, heroic rescuer of puppies, after all.

Mum K and Mum Gen clanked back down the ladder, leaving Sam, Surprise, Sammie and Pea in the attic.

Sam let Sammie have a turn hugging Surprise, and stood up to explore the secret room at last. He stroked the wall, just to see what it felt like; flipped the bare light bulb on and off, just because he could. It felt brilliant.

'It's much bigger than my bedroom,' said Pea, with a sigh. 'I wish mine went all the way back too.'

The attic filled up the whole of the roof space, to make almost two separate rooms: a sloping ceiling at the front and back, and a flat higher ceiling in the middle with a narrower bit of floor, the sticky-out chimney breast taking up half the space. The sloping half at the back of the house looked exactly how Sam thought an attic ought to: dark and dusty, and stacked with luggage and an old tartan picnic blanket; a red tricycle

he vaguely remembered; the old doll's house wedged in a corner, now quite chewed around the chimney; and the other cardboard boxes Mum Gen had decided to keep: *TOYS, LEGO, ETC., PHOTOS 3–6, HOSPITAL.*

But the front half was clean and bright. There was a sloping window set into the roof, just like the one in Pea's bedroom next door, and the walls were freshly painted, in strange misshapen, mismatching squares: yellow, and a slightly different yellow, and a sickly sort of lavender. There were still miniature paint pots on the drip-speckled floorboards. That was the chemical smell, Sam realized, sniffing: new paint.

'Why are they painting up here?' he said, prodding the lavender square dubiously.

'Why do you think?' said Sammie dully.

'Look!' said Pea, unfurling a curly roll of paper. It was a computer drawing of their house, all neat, perfect straight lines, but as if the house had been cut in half – and a floor plan of the attic, like someone had lifted the roof off and looked down. Below it were identical images – but in these, instead of a ladder, the attic had a staircase, just like the one next door. 'They're making it into a proper bedroom like mine!'

She hopped up and tilted the window open, peering out sideways across the roof tiles. Then she ran over to the trapdoor, saying, 'Stick your head out of here – I'll see you in a minute!' and vanished.

Sam looked out of the window. It was the sort that tilted open from the middle: he tipped it up and leaned out, feeling a faint tinge of avocado-ness at the sight of the ground so very far below. He looked up instead. He could see straight across the street to the Bad House. The grim metal panels had been taken down from the top-floor windows now, but there was nothing to see inside: only mouldering old orange curtains, and cracked and filthy panes of glass. It almost looked more sinister, as if the Bad Man might pop his head out at any moment.

Sam shivered, remembering that soft, helpless crying sound.

'Hello!'

His head banged against the tilted window as he jerked backwards, seeing Pea's disembodied head sticking out of the roof only a few metres away.

'Sorry!' she said. 'Didn't meant to be startling. How brilliant is this, though? You *have* to ask for it to be your bedroom.'

Sam smiled. Maybe he did like the idea, now he'd made it up the ladder. It would be like his own *Pocket Rocket*. He could even tell them not to bother with the stairs, so as to make it feel extra spaceship-like.

He pulled his head in. 'Can I, Sammie? You could have my room, if you wanted. We could swap in a year.'

But Sammie was leaning low over Surprise, hugging him close and shaking her head. 'We can't, Sam. That's not what it's for.'

'Why not?'

'Can't you guess?' she said, flinging out an arm.

Sam frowned at the patchwork of squares painted on the attic wall. He stared at the things Mum Gen had decided to keep: the red tricycle, the Lego, the doll's house.

'Are they starting a shop for selling old toys?'

Sammie groaned. 'No, you muppet! It's not going to be a shop. It's going to be a bedroom. Just not for us.'

'For them?' But his mums already had the biggest bedroom.

Sammie was shaking her head again. 'Don't you get it?' she sighed as Surprise jumped out of her arms to snuffle across the floor. She wrapped her arms around herself instead, like a one-person hug. 'We've got too old. They're bored with us. Mum K's going to finish her book and she needs someone else to write about. And she's given up her job in Edinburgh so she can look after it.'

'Is it a horse?' said Sam, frowning at the ceiling. (It was very low. A horse would not like to live up here. It probably wouldn't enjoy the ladder either.)

Sammie shook her head mournfully. 'No, stupid. It's a baby. I think they're having a new baby.'

15

Dear Stupid New Baby,

The Paget-Skidelskys are full.

If you are a girl, we have one of those.

If you are a boy, we have one of those too. See?
(I know he is a bit Sam B and hopeless, but he still counts.)

Also I plan to be a very compelling teenager, and Mum K will be too busy writing books about my international javelining career to bother with you.

This attic could totally definitely fit a horse in it now I've thought about it, so there won't be room for you anyway.

Go away go away go away.

From your not big sister

Poor Sam looked as if Surprise had been dognapped all over again. 'A baby? A whole one?'

He sat down hard on the paint-speckled wood floor.

Sammie sighed. She'd worked it out ages ago: the paint tins, the plans. Sometimes it was tough being the Best Twin, waiting for him to catch up all the time.

'Think about it, Sam. Mum K's come back to live in London all the time because she won't be able to be a mum for a baby only at the weekends. Babies need loads of looking after, and feeding, and staying up all night while they cry. Why else would Mum Gen have wanted to keep all these old toys and things? And they've even bought new ones – look.'

Sammie scrambled up and flipped open the *HOSPITAL* box. There was a soft white rabbit inside, tucked under the scrappy list of baby names Mum Gen had found: pristinely clean, still with its shop tag on. It was obviously brand new.

'That's why they're being all secretive and weird. That's why Mum K needed to talk to that Angel builder woman. They need an extra bedroom, or we'd have to share. That's what the attic's for. Not us. A baby.'

Sammie flopped down on the wood floor too, taking care to avoid the damp patches. Surprise padded over and rested his head on her knee. She stroked his ears sadly.

'Why wouldn't they just tell us?' Sam asked with a frown.

'Ugh, why do you think? They're waiting until it's too late and we can't complain and tell them not to.'

'Do we want to tell them not to?'

Sammie let out a disgusted snort.

Of course they wanted to tell them not to. Babies were terrible. They wailed all the time so no one could sleep; then, when they were asleep, no one else was allowed to be noisy. It was all there in the old note-books – *SAM & SAM: EARLY YEARS* – and Mum Gen's old letters; baby Sammie had once yelled for forty-eight hours without a break, and her eyes had glued themselves shut. And that was before you even got to the sick, and the endless exploding nappies. (They were all in the book notes too, including the time baby Sammie had licked all the pine needles off the carpet under the Christmas tree, resulting in a series of festive spiky poos. Sammie had flushed the offending pages down the toilet, just in case Mum K was remotely tempted to share.) And they took for ever to grow up. Reema's baby sister was only one and a half still, and she'd been born *ages* ago.

'We definitely don't want one,' Sammie said firmly. 'Anyway, they've already got us! We're meant to be enough.' She put her nose close to Surprise's. 'I want to be enough.'

Surprise wouldn't like it if they suddenly got a new puppy. He'd have to behave like a proper grown-up, sensible dog, so they could look after the little one. He'd have to share them. However hard they tried, there would less of them spare to love him.

A new baby would spoil everything.

Sam stood up, looking worriedly at the paint pots. 'Shall we go and tell them we've worked out what the attic's for?'

'No way! If they can keep secrets, we can too.'

Sammie wrinkled her nose, and lifted the stinky puppy up, holding him at arm's length. 'Bath time, you,' she said, clanking down the ladder.

She would let him chew Mum K's hairbrush, just the way he loved.

CAPTAIN'S LOG: TUESDAY

SANDWICH CONDITIONS: CHEEEEESE
BAD HOUSE: STILL BAD
SURPRISE: NOT LOST
LADDER RUNGS CLIMBED WITHOUT
ASSISTANCE OF LOST DOG, WHILE BEING A
FLUFFY CLOUD: 9

CAPTAIN'S LOG: WEDNESDAY

SANDWICH CONDITIONS: JAMMY
BAD HOUSE: STILL BAD
SURPRISE: CONTINUING TO NOT BE LOST
LADDER RUNGS CLIMBED WITHOUT
ASSISTANCE OF LOST DOG, WHILE BEING A
PROFESSIONAL TENNIS PLAYER REGAINING
MY FOCUS BEFORE CHAMPIONSHIP POINT: 10

By Friday, Sam had made it all the way to the top of the ladder, and back down again, three times in a row.

Class Six could talk of nothing but Treetops: what to wear; who would get to sit at the back of the coach on Monday morning; whether there might, in fact, be bees.

Miss Townie let them watch the video of her screaming on the DEATH SLIDE OF DOOM six times over – and this time Sam could imagine himself flying along, with Miss Townie at the top of the ladder beaming with pride and telling him he was *bold and natural, like a rainbow across the sky.*

He waited until the end of school, then slipped up to Miss Townie's desk and handed her a folded sheet of paper.

TREETOPS HOMEWORK QUIZ!

This homework quiz is private. You don't have to share it with anyone except Miss Townie.

My name is: SAM PAGET-SKIDELSKY (THE BOY ONE)

My age is: 11

My best friends are: EVERYONE SAME

AS BEFORE (THOUGH JUST SO YOU KNOW, I CAN
SHARE A BUNK-BED WITH MY SISTER)

Foods I like to eat are: CHEESE
SANDWICHES

Foods I don't like to eat are:
STILL HUMMUS

Foods I'm not allowed to eat are:
COLA DRINKS (MY MUMS SAY THEY MAKE
CHILDREN GO DERANGED)

I am looking forward to: GOING ON
THE RESIDENTIAL TO TREETOPS

I ~~am~~ ^{WAS} worried about: GOING UP VERY
HIGH PLACES (SUCH AS THE TOPS OF TREES,
ALSO LADDERS) AND THEN HAVING TO JUMP OFF
THE VERY HIGH PLACES BECAUSE I DO NOT
LIKE VERY HIGH PLACES. THIS IS CALLED
ACROPHOBIA AND I HAVE IT.

**Is there anything else you would
like your teachers to know?**
I STILL HAVE ACROPHOBIA BUT LUCKILY I'M
BRAVE. I STILL MIGHT NEED YOU TO SAY
HELPFUL AND ENCOURAGING THINGS AT THE
BOTTOM OF LADDERS, TOPS OF LADDERS,
MIDDLES OF LADDERS, ETC., THOUGH, IN CASE I

HAVE A LESS BRAVE FEELING. ALSO YOU COULD
TELL ME TO THINK I'M A SOAP BUBBLE OR
THAT I HAVE LOST MY DOG, AS APPARENTLY
THAT HELPS. THANK YOU.

Miss Townie raised her eyebrows while she read,
then waited until everyone else was busy fetching
their bags and lunch boxes from the pegs.

'Thank you for this, Sam! That's very helpful of
you. Now – I didn't know you were . . . what's
that word? *Acrophobic*. Have you been worrying all
this time?'

'No,' said Sam cheerfully. 'Because I've mostly
been thinking about my dog and also squids and tiny
robot unicorns. And I've been practising, so I know
I can do it. But I haven't had to jump off anything
OF DOOM, so I thought I should tell you.'

Miss Townie smiled fondly, and put the homework quiz in an envelope. 'Thank you for sharing
that with me, Sam. I'll make sure this gets to Mrs
McMin before Monday.'

'Why?'

'Because she's the one looking after you at

Treetops, of course,' said Miss Townie, with a light laugh. She smoothed one hand across her round bump of a tummy. 'I'd love to come – we had such fun last year – but I'm afraid they don't let pregnant people do DEATH SLIDES OF DOOM, or rope bridges. So this year the teachers taking you on the residential will be Mr Vine from Class Four, and Mrs McMin.'

16

SECRET #7:

MRS MCMIN IS EVEN WORSE THAN HUMMUS

'I can't do it,' said Sam miserably. 'I can't go to Treetops.'

Sam, Sammie, Pea and Tinkerbell were gathered in the Paget-Skidelskys' attic for a secret Saturday morning meeting. Tinkerbell – dressed again in wetsuit and wellies, 'Just in case,' despite the bright blue sky outside – was blobbing splotches of paint on the wall from the little tester pots. Sammie was peering out of the window at the deserted Bad House. But Sam was slumped on the freshly scrubbed floor, his chin in his hands, feeling less Samazing by the second.

'But you can do the ladder now,' said Pea, frowning as Tinkerbell smeared a dark purple line across the wall. 'Well, sort of.'

'That was with help!' Sam shouted, loud enough to make Sammie jump and bang her head on the tilted window.

'Ow!'

'Sorry. It's just – I can't . . . It's not just the ladders,' he mumbled.

'It's Mrs McMin,' explained Sammie, screwing up her mouth as if she'd eaten an old sock filled with hummus.

'She's a teacher. She can't be that awful,' said Pea sternly – but she was met by three stony faces. 'Really? Does she hit you on the knuckles with a ruler? Ooh – does she wash your mouth out with soap? I've always wondered what that meant.'

'Teachers aren't allowed to do that,' said Tinkerbell.

'They are in books,' said Pea darkly.

But Tinkerbell shook her head. 'She's much worse than anyone in a book, Pea. She stands over people at hot lunch and won't let them leave until they've finished absolutely all the things on their plate. Once she made my friend Angelo cry over six peas and a baby sweetcorn. We all went out to do PE and we could see them through the window, even though it was after the bell and everything. She just stood there while he put the peas in his mouth one at a time and cried and cried. He had to take the baby sweetcorn home in a Tupperware box and bring it back the next day so she could watch him eat that too.'

Sammie nodded. 'She spits when she talks, and sometimes it lands on your face. And she makes you do PE in the lost-property-box clothes if you forget your kit. Once in Class Three I had to wear an age ten swimming costume with a pink frill on the bum to play cricket.'

'She's just not . . .' Sam crinkled his forehead.

'Kind?' said Pea.

'Nice?' suggested Tinkerbell.

'*Human,*' said Sam. 'I think she might actually be a robot.'

'Imagine her tucking you up in bed at night,' whispered Tinkerbell.

Sam shuddered. 'She gets meaner and shoutier in the afternoons as well. By bedtime she'll probably go full robot. Her eyes will start glowing and she'll

GOOD ROBOT: Ribena-dispensing hatch, instant homework, fun buttons

BAD ROBOT: Rust-gubbins, shoutbox, fearsome hypno-eyes

make us all go to sleep with laser beams shooting out of her earrings. But, you know, not in a good way.'

Pea looked worried. 'Can't you just tell your mums you don't want to go?'

Sam shook his head. 'If I tell her how much I'm going to hate it, she'll make me go even more.'

'Mum Gen says it's character-building to do stuff you don't like. That's why we have piano lessons, because Mum Gen had them and they were awful and it made her the woman she is today.' Sammie's lips pinched up with dismay. 'Anyway, I tried that already, when Miss Townie told me I had to share a bunk-bed with Smelly Nelly.'

The sharing lists had gone up mid-week. Sam was bunking with Halid. Sammie was paired with Nelly, in a dorm with Nishat, Honey, Reema and Emily.

'Does she smell that bad?' asked Tinkerbell, eyes wide.

'Not really,' admitted Sammie. 'Actually I've never given her a proper sniff. It's just 'cos she's called Nelly. I don't like her, anyway. She's boring

6 × 4 = 24

and weird and quiet. She didn't even laugh when I stapled her plaits to the maths display in the shape of a *times* sign last year, and that was hilarious.'

Pea – whose own red hair was in two thick plaits that day – gave her a wary look. 'Does Sme— I mean, Nelly. Does *she* want to share with *you*?'

Sammie narrowed her eyes, but she didn't say

anything; just flicked at a spider dangling from the picnic blanket in the corner.

'Then' – Pea looked apologetic – 'Sam, there's nothing you can do. You have to go.'

Sam felt like Angelo being made to put six peas into his mouth and swallow them down; as if he couldn't breathe at all. Mrs McMin wouldn't under-stand about acrophobia. She wouldn't say patient, helpful things about being a leaf or an eagle. She'd just laugh at him for being slow, shout at him for being scared, tell him he was a girl when he still wasn't one and . . .

'I can't do it,' he murmured. 'I *can't*!'

And he had to lie on the paint-speckled floorboards for a quiet minute doing Attentive Breathing, while Pea read Validating Statements from Mum K's book.

'*I am calm within and without, like an iceberg floating in a cool ocean.*

'*I am a hot-air balloon rising high and proud above the trees.*

'*I am a cloud, drifting steadily in a sunny blue sky.*'

'Is that helping?' asked Pea.

'Not really,' said Sam, sitting up again. 'I don't think I can be all three at the same time.'

Tinkerbell coughed politely. 'Of course it isn't helping. He doesn't need to think he's an iceberg. He needs a *plan*. Luckily, I'm here.'

She produced a rattly tube from her plastic mac pocket, and began to shake it up and down, while humming. 'I'm summoning the wind and the rain,' she explained, between hums.

Sammie squinted out at the blue sky. 'You really aren't. Anyway, Miss Townie said if it rains at Treetops, you just do all the same stuff with a coat on. We need a *real* plan.'

Tinkerbell found a pencil and wrote a list.

PLANS FOR RESCUING SAM FROM CERTAIN DOOM

1) MURDERIZE MRS MCMIN.
2) BREAK SAM'S LEG BEFORE HE GOES.
3) BURN DOWN ALL THE TREES AT TREETOPS
   SO THERE AREN'T ANY LADDERS TO CLIMB.

Pea turned pale. 'You can't kill a teacher! Or break anyone's leg!'

Tinkerbell looked forlorn, and sighed. 'That's

easy, then,' she said, crossing out the first two items on her list. 'Burning down Trectops it is. You'll need some matches, and petrol – there's some in a red can in our shed, for the lawnmower – and some black clothes, so you can sneak out very late at night, and a wet towel to go over your face so you don't breathe in the— What?'

'I think that might be worse than breaking legs,' said Sam as Pea unsuccessfully tried to wrestle the pencil out of Tinkerbell's hand. 'On the posters at school everyone looks really happy. Luanna-Bella says it's the only holiday she's going on this year. Look, I don't want to spoil it for everyone else. Just me.'

Tinkerbell crossed out number three on the list too.

They all stared at the empty line underneath, thinking hard.

Captain Samazing would be able to think of something. A heroic plan! Saving the day! With an explosion in it and things going *BOOOOOOM!* Captain Samazing never gave up.

There was a light clanking noise, some snuffly breathing, then Surprise hopped up through the trapdoor into the attic.

'Hello, daft dog,' said Sammie, scooping him up before he could eat her sweets. 'You aren't meant to be in the attic, remember? Last time you came up that ladder, it was like you'd turned invisible. If Sam hadn't heard you from Pea's bedroom, no one would ever have known you were up here at all.'

Sam's heart began to boom in his chest, and his shoulders swelled. Suddenly he knew exactly what to do.

He picked up Tinkerbell's pencil and added a new plan to the bottom of the list.

4) HIDE SAM IN THE ATTIC.

17

Dear Mrs McMin,

Unfortunately Sam Paget-Skidelsky (the boy one) will be unable to attend Treetops after all. He has ~~bubonic plague~~

~~a sniffle~~

a possible concussion after ~~falling off a ladder like a total muppet~~ a fall yesterday, and doctors have advised that he should remain at home to be monitored for the next 48 hours.

Yours sincerely,

Dr K. Skidelsky (mother)

oo
weird

oo feeble

oo
uch
e a
ing
at might
tually
ppen

'Are you sure you don't want me to come?' called Mum Gen, lingering on the doorstep on Monday morning. 'I could still cancel my first appointment. I'll ring them right now . . .'

Mum K rolled her eyes. 'Waving them off from the front door is exactly the same as waving them off in the playground. I doubt they'll be scarred for life if you aren't there. Will you be scarred for life?'

Sam and Sammie shook their heads firmly – but Mum Gen rushed out and gave them a second round of hugs and kisses just in case.

'Have a wonderful time! Remember to phone us – you have got my old mobile phone, haven't you?'

Sammie rolled her eyes, and produced the battered mobile from her jeans pocket.

Then she threw Sam a querying look, and he nodded once, sharply. Pea's mum's old phone, turquoise with *Little Mermaid* stickers peeling off the back, was stuffed into his backpack, under a week's supply of muesli bars. His sleeping bag, pyjamas, and more snacks were already hidden in the attic, waiting.

'And the pocket money? That ten pounds is to last all week, so don't go spending it all at once. Be completely careful but also utterly adventurous and brave. Sammie, remember to be . . . you know. Nice. Kind. If in doubt, be like Sam. You've got the water-proofs? And jumpers? I know it's glorious now but the forecast's awful later in the week – you need layers – let me just pop upstairs and— Oh, all right, go on, go! I'll see you on Friday!'

Mum K pressed a tissue into her hand. 'You never used to fuss like this when I was leaving for a week. I'm taking it personally.'

Mum Gen erupted into a sob, and Mum K had to steer them off down the path before she could leap in for another round of hugs and weeping.

The Orchid Lane Primary playground was crammed with mums and dads and grandparents and childminders, all carrying brightly coloured backpacks and suitcases. Mr Vine was trapped in their midst, clutching fistfuls of asthma inhalers in clear plastic bags. Mrs McMin stood at the door of the coach with a clipboard, loudly telling Luanna-Bella's mum that no, she could *not* bring a whole suitcase of bottles of Diet Coke, while Nishat's grandfather tried to press twenty pounds into her hand as Bee Protection money. Everywhere people were laughing and yelling and crying. It was chaos.

It was perfect.

Sammie checked her watch: 8.02 exactly.

Time for the plan to begin.

She gave Sam a nudge – he looked nervous and a bit sweaty, but that was good, that was extra-convincing; anyone would believe he'd fallen on his head – and slowly let herself drift into the crowd beside the coach, while Mum K tried in vain to stop Surprise from chewing the wheels of Halid's shiny black plastic suitcase.

At 8.03 precisely, a fuzzy orange carrot rolled under the bus.

Surprise shot after it at once, yelping madly – dragging Mum K behind him and scattering cross mums and dads and grandparents and childminders in her wake.

'Whose dog is that?' said Mrs McMin, nostrils aflare. 'No dogs are permitted on this residential!'

'Sorry, miss!' said Sammie brightly, popping up under her nose. 'My mum said to give you this letter.'

While Mrs McMin fumbled for her reading glasses and tutted, Sammie watched Sam dart round the front of the coach, out of sight . . . Mum K scrambled on the ground, muttering, 'Ridiculous dog,' to herself.

'Hmm. Well, I suppose if you've been given medical advice,' said Mrs McMin coldly. 'We can't give a refund, you know. And if he wants to come along for part of the week, your mother will have to make the transport arrangements herself. It's all *very* inconvenient.'

'Thanks, miss! I bet Sam'll be really touched by all your warmth and sympathy,' said Sammie sweetly as she hopped onto the bottom step. 'Bye, Mum K!'

'Wait!' Mum K shouted, still scrabbling after Surprise's lead. 'I haven't . . . I was going to . . .'

Sammie slipped into the coach, edging along the seats, lost in a sea of waving arms.

The coach doors slid closed.

The engine started.

Mum K waved frantically, mouthing, 'Where's Sam?' through the window as she wrestled Surprise safely out from under the back wheels.

Sammie waved an arm vaguely towards the rear seats, then slotted herself into a seat.

The coach rolled out of the school gates, giving Sammie just a tiniest glimpse of the newsagent's across the road, and a familiar pale face peering out from inside its glass front door.

It had worked.

It had worked.

Sam watched Mum K linger at the school gate, shoulders tilting in the direction the coach had gone as if she'd left her wallet on the bus and wished she could run after it. Then she pulled a tissue out of her pocket, awkwardly wiping her eyes underneath her glasses. A little twist of guilt knotted in his insides – Mum Gen was the mum for crying; Mum K never cried, not even watching *Bambi* – but Mum K shook herself, and began to stride off towards the shops. He used his Treetops pocket money to buy five rolls of wine gums: one for each day of his forthcoming mission.

In the park he found a quiet bench – near the duck pond, with a clear view of all entrances just in case Mum K decided to bring Surprise out for a morning stroll – and practised being a secret.

At 9.37 Sam ate his first roll of wine gums.

At 9.42 a mum with a pushchair sat down next to him and started asking hard questions like, 'Hello, not at school today?' and 'Are you here with one of those mums or dads over at the sandpit?' Sam wasn't sure if she was Stranger Danger – she didn't have a top hat, and the baby in the pushchair looked too smiley to have been Terribly Kidnapped – but he got up just in case and went on to another bench, with the mobile phone clamped to his ear, shouting, 'Marguerite? It's Nigel. I'm in the park!' in a busy-sounding voice.

At 10.01 he opened the next roll of wine gums.

Every now and then the borrowed mobile phone buzzed in his pocket.

Sharks have got the back seat

I am sitting with Nelly

She does not smell of anything actually

She doesn't talk either

I think she may be a mouse in human form

Reema has a butterfly hairclip today

Oliver Baxter has been sick on Honey's shoe and sock and a bit of her leg and now Everywhere smells of sick

Paolo has squirted African Beats deodorant spray all over everywhere

Now everywhere smells like camels and boy

And a tiny bit like sick

Sam smiled to himself. He wasn't missing anything good. The plan was brilliant, and nothing at all could go wrong.

'What happened to Sam?' asked Halid, hanging over the back of Sammie's seat.

'Sit down, Class Six!' bellowed Mrs McMin.

'Is he really not coming at all?' whispered Nishat, meekly peeping out from the seats in front.

'*Well . . .*' said Sammie as every eye on the coach turned her way. 'It was awful. A box fell out of our attic onto his head. A big box. Heavy. With sharp edges.'

'Ooooh,' murmured the coach.

'He was, like, knocked unconscious completely for nearly twenty minutes. Practically a coma. Almost dead.'

'Aaaaah,' murmured the coach.

Sammie detailed her heroic staunching of the blood with a copy of *The Twin Dilemma: the Joys and Challenges of Raising Multiples* until the ambulance arrived. Even Reema and Emily, tucked into the seats at the front with the teachers, peered round to listen, eyes wide.

Not that she cared what they thought.

But still. It felt nice, having all of Class Six actually *wanting* to hear her voice.

'The paramedics told my mums it would've been loads worse if I hadn't been there,' she added proudly. 'He could've been, like, paralysed or something.'

'Whoaaa,' said the coach.

'You're well lucky to have me as a partner,' said Sammie, nudging Nelly's elbow. 'If anything sharp falls on your head, you probably won't even die.'

Nelly let out a small squeak of terror, and edged slightly closer to the window.

Sammie's mobile buzzed in her pocket.

'Is it Sam?' called Christopher, from two rows back.

Sammie nodded.

> This phone is for emergencies only

Another text came swiftly after.

> I have eaten three rolls of wine gums

'He says he's, like, gutted he's missing Treetops,' said Sammie, tilting the screen carefully away from prying eyes. 'And . . . er . . . to tell Nishat not to worry about bees.'

Nishat smiled, and settled back into her seat.

Poor Sam, said the coach. *Poor almost dead Sam.*

Brilliant me, thought Sammie. *Brilliant me, keeping him a secret.*

The coach rolled on down the motorway to Treetops.

> We are here

> We are at treetops

> Gogogo

Sam didn't need telling twice. It was now almost eleven a.m., and he had eaten all five rolls of wine gums, three muesli bars, and all his packed lunch (made by Mum Gen today: cheese again) to fill up the nervous waiting part.

Now that Sammie was safely at Treetops, with no coach explosions (Tinkerbell's worry) or suspicious phone calls from teachers (Pea's more sensible one), it was time for Stage Two of The Plan.

Mission Objective: infiltrate the attic.

Sam walked back towards his house on high alert, checking over his shoulder and running low and close to the parked cars, in case he needed to duck out of sight.

The Heavenly Construction van was parked outside the Bad House, Angel and the leathery man happily distracted by working on the roof.

There was a car parked there too: silver, with DAVECABS printed on the side above a phone number.

Sam hurried past, ducked into the side passage of his house, and let himself in using the silver key from under the pottery fox.

He was in.

Now to get upstairs.

Mum Gen would be in the front room, busy handing out tissues on the golden sofas. Mum K would be in the study, writing about him.

Breathlessly, Sam toed off his trainers – socks would be quieter on the wooden floor of the hall – and stuffed them in his backpack. It had been crammed as full as he could manage that morning, with food supplies to last until Friday, but it already looked suspiciously empty.

He did a quick circuit of the kitchen to top up supplies: apples, crisps, a pot of raspberry yoghurt, a family-sized block of Cheddar cheese. A knife and a plate. There was an open packet of cow biscuits, so he grabbed that too – and put one in his mouth, for tranquillizing purposes.

There was a creak from above, and the sound of a door closing.

Sam heard the familiar patter of Surprise's paws on the stairs, followed by another, heavier tread.

He froze. His teeth bit down, and the end of his cow biscuit fell out of his mouth and broke in two on the kitchen floor.

'Get out from under my feet, you little monster. All right, yes, I'm letting you into the garden right now . . .'

Mum K rounded the bottom of the stairs, and headed for the back door.

In the kitchen.

Where Sam was standing, in his socks.

18

SECRET #8:

SAM PAGET-SKIDELSKY IS HIDING
UNDER THE KITCHEN TABLE

Sam ran jerkily around the kitchen, frantically trying to close every open cupboard and drawn-out drawer as quietly and quickly as possible. There was no time to go out through the back door. Clutching his overflowing backpack, he flung himself under the kitchen table.

There was a clicking of doggy nails on wooden floorboards, followed by a happy growl and a horrible wet sound.

Sam peered out from under the tablecloth, and saw Surprise gleefully savaging the fallen biscuit. 'Good dog,' he whispered.

Surprise's little snout jerked up, and he began to sniffle across the floor, closer, *closer* . . . Oh no no no— But then Mum K's feet arrived in her purple trainers.

'All right, you. I know, I know, you've already managed a magnificent poo in the middle of Homebase this morning – but I know that look. Come on, outside. And let's just check that back gate's shut. I'll not be forgiven if the Sams come home and find you've vanished again.'

Surprise's wet black nose disappeared as Mum K banged out of the back door.

There was no time to waste. Sam hurled himself out from under the table, hugging the backpack, and made for the stairs.

He got halfway down the hall when there was a squeak of a golden door handle, and Mum Gen's voice drifted out of the front room.

'. . . thought you could play a little game together, you and your dad. Something fun, hmm?'

Sam spun on one heel and sprinted for the kitchen – but Mum K was coming back in with a shout of, 'Nope! Stupid dog outside running around barking, clever human inside with a coffee, remember?'

He was trapped.

With a silent yelp, Sam threw himself through the open door of the study, and slid under the big wooden table.

'Just in here, that's right,' said Mum Gen, her Professionally Gentle voice drawing closer. 'Let's try the game with all the roads and castles and fields, shall we?'

The chair Sam was pressed up against suddenly disappeared, tipping him sideways. A moment later it came back, along with a pair of black school trousers, scuffed shoes, and a flash of brown ankle.

Rohan.

There was a clunky sound over his head: Carcassonne game tiles being tipped out of their box. Then Mr Grover's jean-covered legs and Mum Gen's long flowy skirt appeared under the table too, nudging terrifyingly close to his head.

Mr Grover read out the rules, his deep voice buzzing up Sam's spine.

They began to play, oblivious to the Sam sandwiched between their knees.

After a while Mum K came to join the game too, and the space left for Sam got even tinier. She said exactly the things she'd say when she was playing with Sam and Sammie, like, 'Ha! I'm having *all* these fields, ner,' and 'You're not very good at this game, Rohan, are you?'

Sam heard a faint high giggle that he didn't recognize – but Rohan still didn't say anything.

The game went on, and on.

Mum Gen scratched her knee, her hand skimming millimetres from his nose.

Sam crunched himself up smaller and smaller, making himself as invisible as possible. He felt a horrible wet spurt inside the backpack.

'Can anyone smell raspberries?' said Mum K.

She did not look under the table to see if there was a boy and some yoghurt hiding there.

Sam was just wondering if he could reach into his pocket to switch off his mobile phone when there was a low buzzing noise.

Not now, Sammie, please . . .

Not his. Mum K's.

Sam let out a desperate breath.

'Hello? Oh, hi, Bree. Oh, that animal will be the death of me. Sorry, I'll come and drag the beast back where he belongs.' She scraped her chair back, knees disappearing. 'Excuse me, folks. Apparently leaving a puppy in our back garden now means it digs its way into next door to poo next to their washing line instead of ours. In principle I can't complain, but I suppose it isn't all that neighbourly. Back in a tick. Don't nick my field.'

Sam grinned. If Captain Samazing was trapped, you could guarantee that Pointy the tiny robot unicorn would create a distraction. A hero was only ever as good as his sidekicks.

Mum Gen suggested that she and Rohan's dad had a private little chat, back on the golden sofas.

It was his best possible chance.

Sam waited until the front door had banged shut, and Mum Gen's door handle had creaked just so.

Then he rolled out from under the table and stood up, clutching his yoghurty bag.

Rohan's mouth fell open.

He blinked and stared – but he didn't make a sound.

Sam raised one straight finger to his lips: *Shhh*.

Rohan tilted his head to one side and quirked one eyebrow sarcastically. *Duh*.

Sam laughed, and gave him a quick grateful nod. Then he ran out of the study and flung himself up the stairs. He grabbed the pole, and clicked it into place. The ladder noiselessly unfurled.

'*Lily pad, soap bubble, confident eagle,*' he whispered to himself as he clanked breathlessly up the ladder, lifting the backpack up one rung at a time in front of him (he could hear Sammie's voice in his head: *A plate? Why'd you put in a plate, you muppet?*). He threw it inside, then crawled up over the lip of the trapdoor and lay panting on the attic floorboards for a moment. Then he rolled over to pull up the ladder.

Rohan was standing halfway up the stairs, staring curiously up at him through the banisters.

Sam froze, one hand on the pull-up rope, one clinging desperately to the edge of the trapdoor, as the sound of yappy barking and Mum K's growliest voice drifted up from outside, and her shadow loomed in the glass panel of the front door.

Rohan gave him a smile, then raised one finger to his lips. *Shhh.*

Sam grinned back and pulled on the rope.

The front door banged open, the sound of barking floating up the stairs.

But Rohan was back on his chair in the study, and the trapdoor was shut up tight.

19

Dear Nelly,

Congratulations! I am your new Best Friend (temporary appointment for the duration of Treetops).

   Your job is to laugh very loudly at all my jokes and tell everyone how nice I am until Reema remembers all my brilliantness. Also here is a cardigan. I know it is a bit itchy/festive but apparently Best Friends wear them.

   Please do up ALL the buttons.

From Sammie

Nelly was not the most prepossessing of new Best Friends.

She was a solid sort of person, with comfy round limbs and a hamsterish face. Her hair was scraped back into a tiny limp ponytail – revealing six spots on her forehead which, if joined up like a dot-to-dot, would've formed a saucepan like the Big Dipper (not that Sammie would, probably).

Sammie had spent the coach journey interrogating her for Useful Treetops Skills for showing off.

'So, Nelly, have you galloped on horses before? Do you have secret rope-climbing skills? Have you previously stroked ducks?'

Nelly shook her head, and shrank even further away from Sammie with each question, until she was crushed against the window.

'Well, what special talents are you going to bring to this friendship?'

'Er. I can hold my breath for a really long time,' squeaked Nelly, in a tiny voice. 'Also, my name isn't Nelly. It's Nell.' She held up her wrist. There was a gold charm bracelet dangling there, with sparkly letters spelling out NELL.

'It isn't, though,' said Sammie. 'Nell doesn't rhyme with anything.'

A hamster girl who didn't know how to spell her

own name was never going to make Reema jealous. When they got to the shared dorm – a narrow room, with three sets of bunk-beds and ugly curtains with hexagons on – she wouldn't arm-wrestle for the top bunk either.

'You can have it,' said Nell. 'I don't mind.' And she tucked herself into the corner of the bottom bunk, nibbling warily on the half Kit-Kat Sammie had pressed into her hand.

Sammie frowned as she slid her pyjamas under the top bunk pillow. There was no repulsive feeling of spider-legs down her back. She did not want to draw Nell on a pillow and stab it. She was not Nellphobic, she decided, so much as Nellnotinterested.

She would have to find another way to win Reema back.

The rest of Class Six also found the first afternoon at Treetops a challenge.

Nishat did the Nature Walk wearing all the clothes in her suitcase at once as a protective bee-screen, and had to be dunked in the frogspawning pond to avert sunstroke.

Honey's horse saw a snake and bolted, producing a majestic gallop – leaving Honey blinking in the dirt, two hands held out before her as if still gripping the reins.

Oliver Baxter took twenty minutes to pull himself up the slippery wooden platform of the first rope wall, then slid all the way down again, leaving a thin pink line of rope burns down his chin like a weird beard.

Sammie aced it all. She saw a red squirrel (probably, though no one else did and her camera was in her pocket, but still). Her horse – Chances, a brown one with long limbs and a nice face – fitted comfortably under her bottom, and bounced her along in what the horse lady called a 'decent canter' but was plainly galloping.

Look, Sam, she thought. *Look at me being the Best Twin for real.*

Look, Mums.

Look, Reema.

But Reema was watching Emily's neatly cardiganed form bob up and down in the saddle as if Sammie wasn't there at all.

Sam, meanwhile, was settling into his new attic existence.

It wasn't perfect. Surprise might have created Poo Corner over where the red tricycle now stood, but Sam had no intention of doing so – or of using the Tupperware box Tinkerbell had pressed into his hands 'in case of poomergency'. The Ultimate Cheese Sandwich he'd made for dinner (from two slices of cheese, with cheese in the middle) had got raspberry yoghurt on it, as had his pyjamas, and his pencils, and a bit of the floor. And the painty smell made him feel a bit dizzy. (He'd added a few extra streaks, and a sort of view-screen on the chimney breast, to make the attic feel more spaceship-py.)

And he had been *seen* – which made him rather less of a secret than planned.

But everything else was Samazing.

Definitely.

Every now and then the mobile phone buzzed.

> I love treetops

> We made kites

> It is chicken curry for dinner and I
> have got six poppadoms

Sam wrote back:

I had to hide under a table twice but it was all ok
cheese for dinner
I'm not bored

It was only half past six. The sky outside was still bright blue and sunny. There did seem to be quite a lot of day left for being secret in.

Sam made himself another Ultimate Cheese Sandwich, and poked through the rescued piles of new-old stuff in the dusty dark eaves at the back of the attic.

Behind the *HOSPITAL* box with the list of baby names and the snow-white rabbit there were more boxes: photos of Sam and Sammie in the Class Two school play, along with his costume (Christmas Elf, red and green stretchy stuff all hand-sewn by a cross Mum K at midnight – though it was inexplicably tiny now, they must have washed it; he was never that small); Sammie's Interesting Twigs collection, which for some reason Mum Gen had kept, even though it was essentially a box of twigs; and the old doll's house.

Granny Freya had told Sam to call it a 'toy hotel' instead, but it was definitely a doll's house: the sort with a hinged front, so it opened up like a cupboard, and a roof that flipped up like a lid. It looked vaguely like their real house: the front door was blue, with 24 splodged on it, too big, in silver paint; his bedroom walls were stripy. When he opened a wooden wardrobe in the middle bedroom, his whole family fell out: two hand-drawn cardboard Sams with scribbly hair, Mum Gen (a Sylvanian Families Labrador in a dress) and Mum K (a Lego firefighter – well, half of one: Sammie had pulled off her legs and melted them in a fit of fury, after Mum K had refused to let her dig up the rosebush in the front garden and replace it with a cactus).

They were like a memory capsule: forgotten entirely, but suddenly familiar under his hands.

Sam put them into their right rooms. He took a rubber out of his pencil case and drew a smiley face on it, to be a Surprise. He fashioned a new set of legs for Lego Mum K, out of cheese. Then he added a few splodges of paint to the attic, for authenticity.

'I'm not playing with dolls,' he said out loud, just in case there was a ghost. 'I'm just reminding myself what it was like to.'

There was a sound from the landing below, and he clapped his hand over his mouth, suddenly panicked – but it was the phone ringing in the hall.

He risked opening the trapdoor, just a crack.

'It's them, Kara!' yelled Mum Gen. 'Turn that music off! Hello? Sammie? How lovely to hear your voice!'

'Sam? Sammie? Hiya, kids, this is Mum K here too.'

There was a pause.

'Go and fetch him now!'

'What have you been doing, Sammie? How's the bunk-bed situation?'

Another pause.

'Oh good!' said Mum Gen.

'Truly, you're a reformed character,' said Mum K. 'Have you fetched Sam? We'd like to talk to him as well.'

There was a very long silence.

'Not even to hand over a mobile phone?' said Mum Gen. 'Can't you go and ask . . . Sammie? Oh. OK! Love you, darling! Nighty-night!'

'Night-night, sleep tight!'

More silence, then a click.

'Do you think she heard us?' asked Mum Gen, in a wobbly sort of voice.

'Probably not. But she knows.'

'We could call back . . . just to be sure . . . when Sam has got out of the shower . . . I don't like not talking to him.'

'Shush, mother hen. He'll be fine. When have we ever needed to worry about *Sam*?'

The voices faded away.

Sam pulled the trapdoor up with a click.

He did need to be worried about. Not lots; just enough.

The turquoise mobile phone buzzed again.

> Emily wears a long white nightie to bed like an old lady/ghost

> Nell has pyjamas with rabbits on

> Mrs McMin just came to wish us goodnight and ask if we wanted to be tucked in uuuuuuuuuuuuuuuuuurgh

He wrote back:

Then – for practice; for science really – Mum K would find it interesting for her book – he crawled across the floor to the doll's house and tucked each member of the miniature family into bed too.

Sam looked at Whirry Bunny, peeking out of the box of twigs. He thought about the photo in the study of Mum K's big round belly, and the scan Miss Townie had pinned up on the News Board: her little dinosaur. It was hard to imagine one of those inside Mum K; even harder to imagine it growing into a whole person one day. He pictured Sammic, sulking on the painty floorboards. Angry. But . . . a new baby wouldn't just be noisy and poo-ey. When it was bigger, he could teach it things, like how to draw a bat that didn't look like a holly leaf by accident, and how to ride the old red tricycle. They could watch *Tiny Robot Unicorn Friends* together.

Being a big brother sounded OK.

Sam looked at the miniature attic in the doll's house: empty, untouched.

Then he took one of the matchbox sofas out of the living room and turned it upside down, so the inside could slide out, just a little. He poked a hole in his sleeping bag, pulled out a little bit of white fluff, pressed it inside the matchbox and put this in the attic bedroom. He poked through the Interesting Twigs collection, pulled out a small shrunken pine cone, and tucked that into its matchbox cot. Then he fetched the white rabbit from the *HOSPITAL* box and laid it alongside, in case the pine-cone baby was lonely.

'Night-night, sleep tight,' he said.

There was a soft tapping sound through the wall: three knocks.

Pea, wishing him goodnight.

Sam smiled, and knocked back: one two three.

He got into his pyjamas and slipped down the ladder – *I am a storm cloud, striking out across a blue sky* – to clean his teeth while his mums were eating dinner: he could hear the soft clank of cutlery and plates and giggly conversation floating up through the trapdoor before he pulled it shut.

Then he climbed into his sleeping bag, torch propped by his side, to draw.

At some point he fell asleep, because when he woke up again the sky framed by the narrow window was quite dark, lit only by the soft yellow glow of a streetlamp.

He crawled over to the window to tug it closed.

A flash of movement caught his eye: across the road, in the Bad House.

The builders were long gone.

The scaffolding was deserted.

No one was there.

Except . . .

Again, movement, high up on the top floor, at the right-hand window, lit up by a streetlamp.

The mouldy orange curtains hanging down parted for just a moment, as if whoever was inside was determined to stay hidden—

Then he saw it.

A glowing pair of EYES.

Sam was being watched.

20

1 knock – yes
2 knocks – no
3 knocks – I am here, all is well, safe to talk
4 knocks – I need …
then 3 knocks – food
then 4 knocks – a distraction
then 5 knocks – an ambulance, I have been
unexpectedly stung by wasps
4 knocks, a gap, then 1 quick knock – Shh!

Three knocks on the wall on Tuesday morning told
Sam that, at last, Pea was awake.

There was no knock for *Help! Danger!* or *I have seen
some eyes!* so he just knocked loads, for ages, quite fast.
Pea was clever; she'd work it out.

There was a pause.

Then Sam heard a scrape from outside as Pea's attic window popped open.

'Sam?'

Her voice was clear and loud, and undeniably that of someone talking to a secret boy in an attic. Maybe Pea wasn't that clever after all.

Sam frantically knocked on the wall some more, which meant, *Immediately shut up* – but apparently Pea thought it stood for *Talk more and loudly*.

'Sam, what's wrong? Have you changed your mind about hiding?'

There was another pause, then her voice dropped into a loud whisper. 'Is it . . . a poomergency?'

Sam groaned.

A moment later he risked thrusting his arm out of the window, with a note in large capitals.

> ## GO INSIDE!!! I AM BEING WATCHED!!!

Then he pulled his arm back in and lay on the floor, panting.

There was a long pause.

'Sam? Who's watching? I can't see anyone.'

Sam grabbed his pen.

BAD HOUSE
LAST NIGHT
SOMEONE IS IN THERE
PROBABLY A SPY

It was the only sensible explanation. Mrs McMin
had worked out The Plan and sent someone to catch
him out and send him to Treetops in time for the
DEATH SLIDE OF DOOM. Any minute now,
there would be a knock on the door, and two mums
doing their Disappointed faces.

'What a shame.'

'I will have to re-write Chapter Seven: Why Sam B is Certainly Not the Best Twin After All.'

'Um. Sam? Why would someone be spying on
you? No one knows you're there.'

They will now, thought Sam. *They will now there's a*

girl with bright red hair sticking out of the roof talking to herself.

'Look, the builders have arrived. If there was anyone in that old house, they'd notice, wouldn't they?'

Sam raised his head so just his eyes were level with the bottom of the window, and peered out. The Heavenly Construction van was back. The leathery man was already climbing across the roof on a ladder laid flat across the tiles. Angel was on the next level of scaffolding, taking the black boarding off the lower set of windows. A radio played, and she whistled along.

The sky was blue.

The sun was blazing.

Even the Bad House looked like it might not be entirely Bad.

'Sam? Did you eat a lot of cheese sandwiches yesterday? Because my mum says cheese gives you nightmares if you eat it before bed. Sometimes she has it on purpose, to help her dream scary bits of plot for her next book. Once she dreamed a whole chapter where a giant blue sea-slug swallowed all the mermaids and digested them slowly to death in its stomach acid, and it was so disgusting the Dreaditor made her take it out and put in a nicer-sounding monster.'

Sam guiltily eyed the last sliver of cheese on the yoghurt-smeared plate.

'Anyway, I have to go and have breakfast now. Have a nice day!'

There was a click as she shut her window.

Sam listened to the builders' radio, drifting cheerfully across the road.

It had to be the cheese. He must've imagined it. There couldn't be a spy in the Bad House.

He was still a secret.

Christopher put four slices of bacon in an envelope at breakfast. Everyone made you a get well from your head injury card and he was going to post it with bacon in it like a present to you so you didn't miss the bacon because the bacon here is the loveliest but I punched him in the nipple before he could put it in the postbox so there will not be any suspicious giveaway bacon arriving in an envelope.

Say thank you to Christopher. Please don't punch anyone else in the nipple.

Archery!!!

We have an instructor called cameron he is lovely he has a frog hat I love him

Oliver Baxter just shot lovely cameron in the elbow with an arrow.
It went right in
He even cried a bit but in a grown-up man way
I got the first aid kit and helped do first aid and now there is blood under my thumbnail. Nishat says people with arrows in their elbow is worse than bees and Luanna-Bella was sick in a bin. Reema was talking so she didn't notice me being brave but I was.

Sam fetched the paint pots and his pencils, and painted an ambulance on the wall, and a Lovely Cameron with an arrow stuck in his arm. He added a tall tree, and a ladder with thirty-six rungs.

The attic seemed very quiet.

It went on feeling quiet, all day.

The sun blazed through the window.

The radio over the road played the same song three times.

Mum K took Surprise out for a run, and walked home eating a dark chocolate Magnum, which she furtively finished on the pavement outside, tucking the wrapper in next door's bin.

And the mobile phone buzzed cheerily away with all the news from Treetops.

> Chips and sausage and ice cream for lunch

> Trip to a farm!!!
>
> Ducks chickens small horses pigs with hair on rabbits

> Haha Oliver Baxter's farm quiz got chewed by a goat

> They sell hairclips here with sheep on them
>
> I bought two and gave one to Nell because I'm nice

> Nell is allergic to wool and has gone all rashy

Sam started to type replies every now and then, but none of it seemed as interesting as arrows or pigs with hair on.

> Sat on the bit of the floor that still smells of lemon zing

> Moved to sit on different bit of floor and knelt in yoghurt

He painted a farm on the wall, filled with T. Rexes and squids. At lunch time he fetched all the doll's house people and set them out in a circle, for company. But ghostly laughter or Surprise's high cheerful bark kept floating up through the chimney breast, reminding him life was carrying on without him, actual-size.

Even Pea was no help; she knocked on the wall three times after school, and Sam knocked back, but it wasn't much of a conversation.

Sam was lonely.

It was a new, unpleasant sensation. That was the thing about being a twin. It was never only you.

> We put Mrs McMin in the parachute and twirled her around and she almost smiled
> It is big screen movie night tonight with unlimited popcorn

> I have
> I'm

Sam pressed delete, and put the phone down. Then, on impulse, he picked it up again and carefully dialled their house number.

'Hello, Dr Kara Skidelsky speaking?'

'It's Sam,' he whispered, his mouth all felty on the inside, his voice rusty – then remembered he didn't need to whisper. 'I'm – um – I'm phoning you up.'

'Sam! At last! How's it all going? Are you having a brilliant time?'

'Yes. Completely. I – we—' He broke off, and looked at the painted walls and the doll's house family. 'There's been a farm. I've had adventures. And, um . . . I've still got £8.26 pocket money left.'

'Glad to hear it!' came Mum Gen's voice. 'What else have you been doing?'

'Just . . . things,' said Sam. He hadn't really planned what to say. All of a sudden he'd just wanted to hear their voices speaking just to him. But on the phone they sounded tinny, like tiny robot unicorn versions of themselves, and he wasn't sure when to talk and when to listen.

'Eloquent as ever.'

'Shush, Kara – you're useless on the phone too. Sam, it's lovely to hear your voice. Are you eating properly?'

Sam looked at the pile of muesli bar wrappers and the sliver of cheese. 'Mostly . . .'

'And what will you do tomorrow?'

Sam fumbled for the Treetops schedule for Wednesday. 'Um. Ping-pong. Canoeing. And the, er . . . DEATH SLIDE OF DOOM.' He felt vaguely unwell even saying it.

'Lovely, sweetheart. Good luck! Be brave! And remember to brush your teeth before bed, and wash your face, and—'

'He knows how to go to bed, Gen.'

'Yes, all right, I'm fussing. I'm allowed to fuss!

Can you put Sammie on?'

'No. She's, um . . . watching the film.'

Mum K sighed heavily. 'You two are like parallel lines. Tell her to give us a call later, OK? Look after yourself, Sam. We miss you.'

'Miss you. Love you, darling!'

'Love you. Night-night!'

'Bye then,' said Sam, and pressed the red button to cut them off.

Suddenly it seemed very quiet in the attic. He shuffled forward on his bum, and put the pine-cone baby back into bed. 'Love you. Night-night,' he whispered.

Sam was still in his pyjamas, so there was no need to change. He rode the tricycle around the attic a few times – for exercise: a hero must keep fit – then added a few more squids to the farm on the wall.

He read books by torchlight till he was sleepy.

Then he climbed into his sleeping bag and stared out at the dark sky. The Bad House loomed against the stars, gloomy and silent.

He couldn't possibly have seen those eyes last night; not really. Pea was right. The builders would have noticed.

But then again . . . *he* was hiding in his attic.

What if the eyes weren't someone spying on him? What if it was someone like him? Another secret boy, just across the road?

Sam crept closer, focusing intently on the mouldering orange curtains.

A few cars drove by.

Then one rolled up the street very slowly, and slid onto the crumbly concrete drive.

Silver, with DAVECABS printed on the side.

A solid figure slid out of the driver's seat. He was dressed all in black, from head to toe, but when he looked up, framed in the glow of the streetlamp, Sam recognized the flash of white teeth and the single curl of shiny hair at once.

Mr Grover.

Sam gritted his teeth anxiously. He should warn him; he should find a way to let him know that it was the Bad House he was parking outside. In the dead of night. Pulling up his hood and furtively looking around as if trying to make sure no one saw him.

Mr Grover reached into the car and pulled out a heavy-looking sports bag. There was a flicker of torchlight from his hand. Then, checking up and down the street again, he walked up to the Bad

House front door, took out a key and let himself inside.

Sam gasped, watching helplessly as the old door swung shut. He caught a few glimpses of torchlight at the second-floor windows, from inside the house. Then, after an agonizingly long time, the front door swung open again, and Mr Grover came out, the bag in his hand now plainly empty.

Sam watched his eyes track across the road, and then slowly travel up the Paget-Skidelsky house.

With a yelp, he ducked down below window level, pressing himself close to the wall.

By the time he felt he could risk peering out again, the silver car was already heading away down the street.

Up on the top floor, the curtains twitched, and Sam caught another flash of eyes, peeping desperately out of the Bad House.

The Bad House, where the Bad Man lived.

21

Dear Reema,

Honey snores loads, doesn't she?

I had three pieces of garlic bread at dinner last
night — did you see?

Remember that time you came to my Family Day
Out and we went to Parliament Hill swimming pool
and Surprise tried to swim by running along the
bottom of the pool?

Did you know there isn't a Dog Tooth Fairy?

Did you know my brother is hiding in the attic in
my house?

Did you know my mums are having a new baby?

Would you like to know? Would you like me to
tell you?

Hello?

There were six missed calls on the mobile phone when Sammie woke up on Wednesday morning.

Probably a poomergency.

Sam would have to sort it out by himself, anyway; Sammie had much more important things to think about.

The Treetops schedule for the day read:

Breakfast

9 a.m.	Badminton
10 a.m.	Ping-pong
11 a.m.	Fencing
12 noon	Canoeing on Treetops Lake

Lunch, rest time

3.30 p.m.	Rope-bridge challenge
4.30 p.m.	The Death Slide of Doom

Dinner

7 p.m.	Treetops Disco!

It was filled with opportunities for her to be quite brilliant and Sam A-like.

Unfortunately she appeared to be the only member of Class Six who had received it.

Nell's schedule apparently read:

Breakfast

9 a.m.	Hit shuttlecock into net; walk to net to pick up shuttlecock; walk back; repeat for one hour
10 a.m.	Mainly pong
11 a.m.	Being pinned against the wall by a girl with a sword while whimpering
12 noon	Despair in a lifejacket

Sammie would've seized the opportunity to appeal to Mrs McMin for a new partner – a girl; perhaps a girl with long dark hair in a ponytail – but Reema's schedule was even more baffling.

9 a.m.	Staring at Paolo
10 a.m.	Staring at Paolo
11 a.m.	Whispering, giggling, staring at Paolo
12 noon	Canoeing on Treetops Lake – while staring at Paolo

She wasn't the only one.

Emily was staring at Paolo too. Now she'd noticed it, Sammie realized that all the girls were. And some of the boys. Even Mrs McMin lowered her Kindle during Fencing, and peered over the top of her spectacles as he did a sort of stabby dance in Alfie's general direction.

Sammie tried staring at Paolo, just to see.

She didn't get it.

He had swoopy hair with spray on it, and big teeth, like someone off the telly – but he wasn't actually someone off the telly. He had nice clothes, she guessed: one of those muscly vest tops with huge armholes so you could see extra parts of him, long football shorts and trainers – but you could just buy those yourselves and wear them and look in the mirror. He seemed to be quite good at paddling a canoe – but no more so than Halid, or Honey, or Christopher.

It was like one of those Magic Eye pictures where, if you squinted, all the blobs turned into a dolphin – except no matter how hard she scrunched up her eyes, Paolo remained just a boy who smelled of camels.

She tried squinting at Emily too.

Still a girl in a cardigan.

Nell: still whimpering.

Reena: still sharing a canoe with someone else, and not noticing Sammie at all.

A chill wind began to ripple across the lake.

Raindrops began to pitter-pat on Sammie's life-jacket as clouds rolled in across the blue skies.

'Can we go in now?' asked Nell, in a small voice.

'Nope,' said Sammie, plunging her paddle into the water, propelling them forwards.

Sam A did not give up.

22

SECRET #9:

MR GROVER IS ACTUALLY THE BAD MAN

Back in the attic, Sam was under siege.

After fretfully watching the Bad House all night, he was suddenly jolted awake by what sounded like someone peeling the roof off the house with a tin-opener.

CLANK!

CRRRK!

SCREEEEEK!

Sam bolted upright. The attic was flooded with daylight and meltingly hot; his hair was sticking sweatily to his forehead and his pyjamas to his back.

He hadn't meant to fall asleep. It didn't seem

very heroic. But then again, he'd never seen a super-hero yawn. They must all be getting a good eight hours' kip in between squids.

A shadow fell across the window.

There was another almighty clatter from above, then something slid across the roof tiles, right over his head.

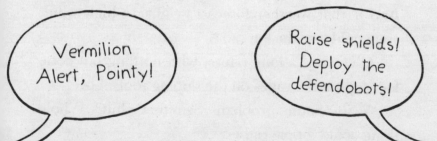

(That meant grabbing the sleeping bag and hiding under it, tucked in tight underneath the window.)

'How's it looking?' came Mum K's voice, floating up from far below.

A shape moved across the window, blocking out the light except for one small crack.

'Gutters need a bit of clearing, but your tiles look sound,' came a woman's voice, directly above Sam's head.

He risked a peek.

It was Angel. He could see two yellow bunches under a hard hat, and a red-and-blue checked shirt just disappearing out of view as she climbed across their roof.

'It's the chimney stack I wanted to check,' she called, her voice muffled and higher up. 'We took the caps off the one over the road last night, found it wasn't properly pointed – not secure, you know? And if that weather forecast's right . . . high wind, you could lose the lot . . .'

There was a long pause, with nothing but eerie footsteps and scrapes on the sloping roof above.

'Yeah. Same problem. See that shift? Whole thing could topple right over.'

That didn't sound good.

'Blimey. Can you fix it?'

That didn't sound good either. Sam couldn't stay under a sleeping bag till Friday while builders crrked and clanked their way across the roof.

But Angel let out a low whistle as her boots appeared one by one, climbing down past the window. '*We* can't. Best I can do is put you on to a few mates, see if anyone's got a free day. Or you could risk it. It's lasted this long. Just didn't want to leave you in the dark.'

She rapped on the window, right above Sam's head, and pressed her face against the glass.

Sam stared frantically around the attic: the doll's house in the middle of the floor, the spaceship view-screen painted on the wall, the dirty plate surrounded by crisp packets and cow biscuit crumbs. In the daylight, it looked suspiciously like there was a eleven-year-old boy living in it.

But Angel seemed oblivious. 'Yeah. Be nice in there, once it's done. Plenty of light.'

There were more scrapes and clanks.

Then, at last, silence.

He hadn't been seen.

Not by Angel, anyway.

The eyes at the window last night . . . whoever they belonged to, he was sure they must have seen him. And he had a feeling that the person had wanted to be seen too.

But who was it?

What did they want him to do?

And what did Mr Grover have to do with it?

Sam looked queasily at the pages of *Captain Samazing vs the Squids of Mars*, scattered in the Entertainment Zone; at the bulgy muscles of his grinning hero.

There was no getting round it. Only the Bad Man would have a key to the Bad House. Only the Bad Man would slip inside, in the dead of night, to check on his victim. Sam would have to tell Miss Townie that the *Stranger Danger* poster he'd made was useless. A Terrible Kidnapper could turn out to be a nice smiley dad from Australia all along.

Poor Rohan. Was it him, locked inside the Bad House, desperately peeking out to catch Sam's eye? Was that why he'd drawn his old house in Australia, not the new one?

And Sam was the only one who knew. The only one who could save him.

It was no use knocking on the wall: Pea would have left for school already.

Instead, Sam grabbed the mobile phone. It took three tries, but at last Sammie answered.

'What?' she demanded. 'I am in the middle of canoeing. And Oliver Baxter's already fallen in twice, and me and Nell had to rescue him, so if you distract me and he drowns, I am telling everyone it was your fault.'

'It's important!'

'Is it . . . a poomergency?'

Sam groaned. Everyone was far too interested in his bottom. 'No! Danger! Bad Man! Bad House! Kidnapping!'

'Go away until you make sense,' Sammie said, and hung up.

This time it took five tries to get her to answer again.

'OK, we are getting changed now. But be quick, because it's pizza for lunch.'

Sam whispered the shortest, simplest explanation he could muster.

Sammie whistled through her teeth. 'Wow. And I thought canoeing was good.'

'It's not good! It's a dangerous emergency! And I'm going to do a heroic rescue – so I'm just letting you know, in case something goes wrong.'

'Cool.' Then Sammie paused. 'Wait! You can't go in the Bad House – you might get murderized. Or kidnapped as well. Anyway, you have to stay a secret or I'll get sent home to be told off, and Reema hasn't had enough time to notice me being brilliant and Best Friendly yet.'

'Oh.'

'You can't give yourself away. You mustn't be seen. What you need to do is—'

The phone went dead.

Sam pressed all the buttons. He hit it against the painty floorboards. But nothing happened.

It was out of charge.

And he didn't have a charger – or any sockets up here to plug one into.

This kind of thing *never* happened to Captain Samazing.

Reluctantly, Sam settled in to wait.

Dear Squids,

Can you please invade after 4:30 pm? I have to wait for my friend to get home from school.

Love
Captain Samazing

It was an agonizingly long day.

The builders played their radio and climbed the scaffolding, oblivious to what was hidden within.

Unhappy people came and went.

The blue skies began to fade, giving way to thick clouds and gusts of wind.

Sam waited, plotting and planning, until he saw Mum K take Surprise out for an afternoon stroll, waving another pair of unhappy people in to see Mum Gen on her way out.

Then he seized his chance.

Barefoot, still in his pyjamas, Sam sped down the ladder, through the kitchen, out of the back door – and, by climbing onto Sammie's old bike, over the wall and into the Llewellyns' garden. Usually it was a flat rectangle of grass, with flowerbeds along the sides – but there was now a large hole in the middle of the lawn, with a mound of earth beside it and a spade sticking out.

Perfect.

Sam crept towards the mound, using it as cover as he peered into Pea's kitchen. It was almost four; she'd be back from school any moment.

The back door flew open, and Wuffly came

charging out, barking cheerfully, followed by Pea's mum.

'Don't you dare go mud-rolling again, Wuffs!' she called, pulling sheets off the washing line as the grey clouds overhead began to spit with rain. 'And if you do, this time wipe it off on Tink's bed, not Clover's . . .'

Sam dived into the pit head first and rolled into a ball.

Wuffly bounced over and followed him in at once, licking his face. Sam crouched lower, but he couldn't help grinning as he ruffled her ears fondly, burying his face in her quivery body. It felt good, having something to hug again; feeling another warm thumpy heart.

He reached into his pyjama pocket and produced a note.

BACK GARDEN
URGENT ASSSISTANCE REQUIRED!
CAPTAIN SAMAZING

It was the perfect secret message. Even if some-one else saw it, they'd never guess it meant him.

'Find Pea,' he whispered in Wuffly's hairy ear, tucking it into her collar and giving her a push out of the hole.

His heart beat faster as he heard Clover humming to herself in the kitchen – then Pea's mum again . . . then there were running feet, and Tinkerbell's head (under the yellow rain hat, as usual) appeared over the lip of the hole.

She gasped, then disappeared.

A moment later she and Pea dropped into the hole beside him, crouching low too.

'What are you doing out of the attic?' asked Pea, eyes wide with worry.

'And why are you in pyjamas?' asked Tinkerbell, crinkling her nose.

Pea was more sympathetic. 'Poor Sam. He hasn't been able to have a wash or anything.'

'I don't need a wash,' he said.

Pea looked him up and down, unconvinced.

He was a bit painty, he supposed, and he had knelt in yoghurt quite a few times. And now he was pretty muddy too. But Captain Samazing did not stop for laundry. 'Who cares? I'm on an urgent mission. And I need your help!'

He explained all about Mr Grover, and him arriving in the dead of night, and the secret kidnapped person trapped in the Bad House.

'Did you have cheese sandwiches before bed again, Sam?' asked Pea.

He shook his head. 'No. Anyway, this started ages ago. Don't you remember when we went hunting for Surprise? Wuffly knew something was wrong. I heard that crying noise inside. Mr Grover was probably bringing his victim some more food, so they won't die.'

Tinkerbell's eyes grew wider and wider as he spoke. 'Wow. I can't believe there actually is a Bad Man. Does he know you saw him?' she said eagerly. 'Is he going to climb up through your window and kidnap you too?'

'Course not. He's enormous – my window's much too small for him to fit through. And he didn't see me. He didn't even look up. I am still totally a secret.'

Pea was frowning. She turned on her most Professionally Gentle voice. 'Sam, is this all real? Not a story to stop you feeling a bit bored. *Really* real?'

'Yes! I keep telling you!'

'Then . . . if someone really has been kidnapped

by Mr Grover, we have to call the police.'

Sam gripped her wrist. 'No! Then I'd have to tell my mums I'm in the attic, and Sammie would have to come home from Treetops, and everything would be ruined. *Anyway* – no one would believe me. You didn't. I told you I saw eyes, and even you said I was making it up.'

Tinkerbell stared at Pea accusingly as Pea turned faintly pink.

'I've been thinking about it all day. What I need is *evidence*.'

Tinkerbell blinked. 'Evidence of what? Didn't the kidnapping bit already happen?'

'I need something to prove there's someone up there. And – he'll have to come back again, won't he? He might even be planning another kidnapping.' Sam held out the turquoise mobile phone. 'This can take photos, right? I just need to charge it up.'

'We can do better than that,' said Pea, taking the phone. 'Mum's got a camera – a proper zoomy one. We'll lend you that too. Anything else?'

'Food? All I've had today is cow biscuits.'

Tinkerbell looked dreamy-eyed at the prospect

of a life led on nothing but cow biscuits, dressed in one's pyjamas.

'OK. Stay here in the hole. Tink, stand guard.'

Pea and Tinkerbell both clambered out.

Sam could hear Tinkerbell marching up and down, singing a song about weather and rattling her rain-stick.

The clouds above grew darker still. The air grew chilly. The rain grew heavier.

'Tink? How are you doing that?'

Tinkerbell's beaming smile appeared over the edge of the hole. 'Magic. I set fire to a painting of the sun yesterday, and now everyone says there's going to be a massive storm tonight. That's why I started digging the swimming pool. It'll probably be full up by tomorrow.'

Sam wasn't sure that was how swimming pools usually worked – or rainclouds – but he was grateful for the hiding place.

At Treetops they'd be on the DEATH SLIDE OF DOOM.

Right now.

Right now this second, Sammie or Alfie or Oliver Baxter would be at the top of that ladder . . .

Reaching out . . .

Stepping off . . .

He shivered. Being in a muddy hole in the rain wasn't exactly Samazing, but there were worse things.

After almost an hour Pea jumped back into the hole – with hot buttered toast, a camera, and a freshly charged mobile phone.

'Are you *sure* you don't want a wash?' asked Pea while Sam wolfed down toast.

He shook his head. 'Thanks!'

With Tinkerbell keeping watch, Sam scrambled out of the hole and levered himself over the wall with a boost from Pea's bent knee. He rolled, and dropped down into a crouch, holding the camera close to his chest.

Keeping low, he ran across the grass to the back door.

He tipped up the pottery fox.

The key was gone.

23

Dear Mum Gen,

You know how you said I should pack jumpers? I did not actually pack any jumpers.

Brrr.

From Sammie

While Sam was worrying about chargers and hiding in a hole, back at Treetops, the fluffy grey clouds had already turned an ominous black.

The tall trees swished as rain began to fall again: not light raindrops this time, but cold, heavy splashes.

'Can we go indoors?' asked Luanna-Bella, shivering in a T-shirt.

'Will we have to do fencing again instead?' asked Nell nervously, eyeing the swaying rope bridges above.

'Nonsense,' said Mrs McMin, zipping up her

anorak. 'Children do not shrivel when wet.'

But half an hour later Class Six were looking distinctly shrunken.

And muddy.

And not especially fond of rope bridges.

The ropes squidged under their cold hands. The wooden boards grew slippy. A case of acute acrophobia was rapidly spreading through the ranks.

Mrs McMin and Mr Vine watched from under a dripping tree, sipping tea from a flask as various squeaks and yelps of terror resounded through the woods.

'Can we go in *now*?' asked Luanna-Bella, looking faintly blue.

'But it's the DEATH SLIDE OF DOOM next!' protested Sammie.

That was what would do it, she was sure: her chance to prove to Reema once and for all that she was brave and fun and better than Sam, better than Emily, better than everyone ever. Death Sliding in the lashing rain would only prove it all the more.

But when they skidded up the muddy slope to the tallest tree at Treetops, Lovely Cameron was waiting, shaking his head.

'Sorry, gang. No Death Sliding today – too windy!'

'Oh dear,' said Nishat wanly.

'What a pity,' said Halid, looking up and up and up.

'Ah well,' said Alfie as the wind whipped the zip-wire around and the clouds spun across the sky.

Treetops' wet-weather programme involved basket-weaving and board games, all their wet muddy shoes jumbled up in the doorway of the Craft Centre.

Sammie's mobile whirred in her pocket. 'What? I'm winning at Monopoly.'

'I'm in a hole in the ground!'

Sammie abandoned her hotel on Park Lane, and went to lurk behind a rack of damp coats as Sam explained why he was not a secret boy in an attic but, in fact, back in the Llewellyns' garden, hiding in Tinkerbell's future swimming pool.

'You can't stay there! You'll get seen.'

Sam agreed, squeakily. 'But I'm locked out!'

'Get Pea to save you?'

'I tried! But Clover answered the phone and I couldn't think of good reasons for her to find Pea so I just hung up. And Pea's mum is in the kitchen! I've got to get back into our house, Sammie. I left the ladder down – if anyone goes upstairs they'll know everything! Also this hole is actually filling up with water.'

This was the problem with the whole attic plan: Sam B was the one doing it. A Sam A would never have got herself locked out. But then a Sam A would never have needed to hide in an attic because of being scared of a big tree, either.

Sammie sighed, and instructed Sam to hang up and wait.

After finding the key missing, Sam had gone back to Tinkerbell's swimming pool, and waited, and waited.

Eventually the back door of Pea's house banged open, and a moment later Tinkerbell's face appeared, peering down into the hole.

She gave Sam a confused look, then vanished.

Another five minutes went by. Then a scrumpled ball of paper bounced into the hole, landing in the muddy puddle that was forming under Sam's cold bare feet.

WAIT TWO MINS
THEN CLIMB OVER THE WALL
WE WILL LET YOU INTO YOUR HOUSE

Sam counted to sixty, twice, then – with one quick glance at Pea's mum in the kitchen – rolled out of the hole. He slithered over the garden wall, dropping low in the squelchy grass.

The back door of his house swung open, revealing Pea's worried face.

'No, really, Dr Skidelsky, we don't mind the rain! We're taking Wuffly for a walk anyway, so Surprise might as well come too!' she shouted over her shoulder, beckoning Sam frantically.

Sam hurried over to the back door, scooping up the camera he'd left safe and dry behind the pottery fox.

'Thanks,' he hissed, shivering as Pea pulled the door closed behind him.

Out in the hall he could see Surprise, barking joyfully around Tinkerbell's ankles, and the back of Mum K's head peeking out of the study.

He took a step forward, but it left a splotch of brown on the kitchen floor, shaped worryingly like the footprint of an eleven-year-old boy who was supposed to be sixty-three miles away.

'Here,' whispered Pea, grabbing up a jumper from a pile of clean laundry on the kitchen table.

Sam rubbed his feet on it guiltily (it was Mum

Gen's, a fuzzy blue one she was fond of), then tucked it under his arm.

Pea sped into the hall. 'Found it!' she said, brandishing Surprise's toy carrot.

The front door banged behind them.

The study door closed.

Wrapping the phone and camera in the mud-streaked blue jumper, Sam raced down the hall, up the stairs, up the ladder and in.

He pulled the ladder rope.

The trapdoor clicked shut.

Soaked and filthy, Sam lay on the painty floor-boards, trying to catch his breath.

Too close.

He rolled over, throwing the ruined jumper aside and placing the camera and mobile phone carefully on his sleeping bag. Then he pulled off his soggy pyjamas and hunted out the hoodie and jeans he'd worn on Monday.

There was a rustling sound.

Sam froze.

He stared at the wall – but this wasn't an echo up the chimney; it was far too close. Sam edged nearer, eyeing the open doll's house. He gave the pine-cone baby a wary prod. It was still just a pine cone.

But the rustling sound came again: over in the darkest corner, by the stack of boxes and the red tricycle.

'Surprise?' said Sam hopefully.

But no: Surprise had been downstairs, being led off on a walk with Wuffly.

It couldn't be the dog.

Another rustle.

The picnic blanket draped over the pile of wheelie cases was *moving*.

Something was underneath.

Something alive.

Tinkerbell's words rang in Sam's ears: *Does he know you saw him? Is he going to climb up to your window and kidnap you too?*

Swallowing hard, Sam pulled his hoodie over his head, grabbed his torch and raised it like a weapon, ready to fight. He reached out with his other hand, took hold of the blanket and threw it back.

It wasn't the Bad Man.

It was Rohan.

24

SECRET #10:

THERE ARE TWO SECRET BOYS HIDING IN THE ATTIC

Sam leaped back, tripping over the doll's house and landing with a thump, the torch clattering to the floor. 'Why are you – how did you – *what?*' he yelled.

Rohan's scrawny shoulders jerked at the noise. He cowered back into the dark corner, clutching the edge of the picnic blanket like a shield and chewing his bottom lip.

'Sorry!' hissed Sam. 'I just . . . You scared me. A bit. More like surprised, really. How did you get in?'

Rohan fumbled under the blanket, then grinned, and held up a silver key; the one that lived under the pottery fox.

'So you just climbed up here and hid and—'

Outside in the street, an engine roared. A car was speeding along terrifyingly fast, screeching to a halt right outside. A second later there was a sudden hammering on the front door, and loud frantic yelling on the doorstep.

'Dr Paget? Hey – are you there, Dr Paget?'

Rohan made a soft squeaking sound, and disappeared under the picnic blanket.

Sam scrambled over to the window. Outside, the silver DAVECABS car was parked at an angle, sticking out into the wet road. Mr Grover was on the doorstep, thumping the door with his meaty fists. He'd just begun climbing into the rose bushes to press his face to the window when he suddenly darted back to the front door.

Don't answer, Sam whispered inside his head. *Pretend to be out. Don't let him in.*

'Thank God. Is he here? Rohan? Is he with you?'

'I'm sorry, why would . . . ? It's rather late and I'm with another client. What's happened?'

'He was in his room – I only left him for a minute – he was in the house and then – he's wandered off somewhere and – you know, it's a long way to here

234

from our place but we've only been here a month, he hardly knows a soul, and—'

The rest was lost as Mr Grover was beckoned inside by Mum Gen's most soothing voice.

They heard voices echoing up from below, and doors opening and shutting.

'Rohan? Rohan, are you here?' came Mum K's muffled voice from the landing beneath them. 'He wouldn't come upstairs, would he?'

'Doubt he'd come here at all, to be honest.' That was Mum Gen. 'It's not exactly his favourite location. But the poor man's frantic; we have to make sure. Hmm . . . you don't suppose . . . Surprise got himself stuck up there . . .'

They were right under the trapdoor. Sam could picture them both, staring up, wondering whether to look inside.

Rohan pulled the blanket off his head, eyes wide and frightened, and held his finger upright across his lips. *Shhh.*

Sam was desperate to drop the trapdoor and warn his mums – but there was no way he was handing Rohan back to the Bad Man. He put one finger to his lips too, and held it there, breathless, watching the trapdoor, willing it not to open.

But it stayed shut. The sounds of doors opening and closing, and Rohan's name being called, faded away to nothing.

Sam let out a long breath. 'It's OK. You're safe here,' he whispered. 'I know your dad's an evil kidnapper – but it's all right. You've escaped now, and I'm going to catch him, and you never need to be scared of him again.'

'What?' said Rohan. 'My dad's not a kidnapper, he's a geriatric nurse.'

Sam scooted backwards. 'Whoa!'

Rohan scratched his nose. 'All right, he's a taxi driver at the moment. But only 'cos we've just moved here. He'll be a nurse again soon.'

Sam stared. Rohan had the same accent as his dad, and a surprisingly low, husky voice. But it was clear as a bell. 'No . . . I mean . . . you can talk?'

'Oh. Yeah.' Rohan shrugged off the blanket and flashed him a grin. 'Duh! I can talk. I just can't *always* talk.' His grin faded. 'It's complicated.'

Sam nodded slowly. Mr Grover wasn't the patient after all; it had been Rohan all along. All the big smiles and gentle questions around the table in the study: they must have been trying to get him to feel at home, and relaxed enough to join in. It made sense. After all, supervillains rarely asked for help on a golden sofa.

'So – is that why you come here? To see my Mum Gen – Dr Paget?'

'Right. She says it's anxiety. I get anxious – like, *super* anxious – and then words won't come out. She calls it selective mutism. I call it annoying.'

Sam nodded in a knowledgeable, Mum Gen sort of way. 'I get anxious too. I have acrophobia. That means a fear of heights. I can do ladders now, but I have to think about it. And it helps if no one's watching.'

Rohan sniffed. 'Me too. Not ladders – the watching thing. If there are strangers or lots of people, usually I can't say anything at all. People keep trying to make me. But that makes it worse.'

Sam nodded sympathetically. 'So . . . does your dad get cross with you for not talking? Is that why he locks you up?'

'Eh? Why would he lock me up?'

'It's not your fault, Rohan. He's a Bad Man. But I'll keep you safe.'

Rohan scrunched up his face. 'You're being weird. Don't be weird or I'll go back down the ladder and tell everyone you're hiding.'

'Hey!' Sam gripped his torch tightly, alarmed. 'It's my attic! You can't do that!'

'You keep saying my dad is an evil kidnapper!'

'Well, actually he is!'

Sam explained all about the Bad House, and the eyes at the window, and Mr Grover letting himself in.

Rohan scrunched up his face even more. 'I don't live behind a mouldy curtain across your street, I live at my nana's flat in Brent Cross. And it's not a Bad House, it's *our* house. Or it will be. They're just fixing it up before we can move in – that's why he's got a key. And my dad's not bad. He's normal. Like a dad.'

'Well, why are you hiding from him then?'

'I'm not! Why are you hiding from your mums?'

'I'm not!'

'Well, duh.' Rohan stuck his tongue out, and folded his arms as if he'd won.

'I think I preferred you when you couldn't talk,' muttered Sam.

Rohan's face went still. Then he put the picnic blanket over his head and sank back into the corner.

'Sorry,' said Sam. He truly was. It was nice, having someone narky to talk to. Sammie argued

238

with him at least six times a day. He missed that.

He fetched the cow biscuit packet and waggled it under the edge of the blanket by way of a truce.

Rohan took one, and pulled the blanket back down to eat it.

'You nibble round the cows too!'

'Doesn't everyone?' said Rohan, biting carefully.

They munched in silence.

'So are you getting better, then?' asked Sam. 'Because of my Mum Gen? Is that why you can talk to me?'

Rohan shuffled inside the blanket. 'Not really. I've met you before; you were nice to me – you drew me pictures – you didn't mind that I didn't talk. And there's only one of you. Not like at school.' He swallowed hard, as if the word *school* tasted like a hummus sandwich. 'I don't talk at school at all.'

'Is *that* why you came up here?'

Rohan nodded. 'My old one back home wasn't so bad,' he said, fiddling with the edge of the blanket, his voice dipping to a whisper. 'The teachers all knew. They let me have a whiteboard in lessons, so I could join in and answer questions, or whisper them to a friend. But now we've moved here, it's all different. I haven't got any friends to whisper to.'

Rohan had nibbled his biscuit down to a tiny cow. He sat staring at it, resting in his palm. 'Is it OK if I stay? 'Cos I could climb back down if it isn't. I could pretend I'd hidden under your bed or something. Only Mr Pepper – he's my teacher – he's making us do an assembly on Friday and he says I have to start it and stand up in front of everyone in, like, the whole school. I'm meant to say: *Good morning, everyone. Welcome to the Year Four assembly. Our topic this month is the Amazonian Rainforest.* Then everyone comes running on doing parrot noises – but . . . it's not going to happen. I can't do it. I'll actually just fall down and die. In assembly. In front of everyone.' His voice went tight and whispery. 'Can I stay here?'

The wind outside swirled, spattering rain against the window.

Sam looked at Rohan's quivery hands, and imagined his own, trying to climb up the ladder to cling to the DEATH SLIDE OF DOOM in front of his whole class, while Mrs McMin watched.

He'd thought he was rescuing a kidnap victim from the Bad Man – but this was just as heroic.

'Yes,' said Sam. 'You can stay. You can be a secret attic person, just like me.'

25

Dear Mum Gen,

You told me if I got stuck, I should Be Like Sam.

I don't think this was very helpful advice when I have to get dressed for a disco with a load of girls, because he doesn't know how to do that either.

Also I did not pack any 'disco clothes' and you didn't tell me to (or what 'disco clothes' are), so actually that is your fault.

I am unprepared for life.

You are both the Worst Mum.

From Sammie

Mrs McMin sent them back to their dorms to 'get ready' a full hour before the disco was due to begin.

As far as Sammie was concerned, 'getting ready' meant putting on some shoes.

That was not what it meant.

Emily's swishy hair turned out to be the result of hanging upside down off the bed over a hairdryer for twenty minutes.

Honey sprayed herself all over with a bottle that made her smell like cake.

Nishat drew around her eyes with black goo.

No wonder everyone was so scared of going up to Year Seven, if this was what the future was going to be like. There wouldn't be time left over for anything fun/violent at all.

'Aren't you going to change?' whispered Nell nervously, looking Sammie up and down, and plucking at her own flippy little skirt.

Sammie *had* changed: from damp muddy jeans to dry, slightly less muddy jeans, and a stripy T-shirt that didn't have garlic bread on it. The only other clean thing in her suitcase was the rejected Christmas cardigan – and even Sammie knew that was wrong. Not in a good way: purposeful, loudly announcing its wrongness, the definition of cool. Just wrong.

On the other side of the dorm, Reema shimmied into a pair of mud-free skinny jeans, and a floaty sort of top with silver beads sewn onto it. She swished her hair up into a ponytail. She looked . . . pretty. Still like Reema; still like her best friend. But like someone else too. Someone old, and new, viewed from the end of a long tunnel.

It was strange, this new feeling.

Doubt.

Sammie couldn't javelin it away. She couldn't shout at it until it cried. It would not be hit.

It was no use being the Good Twin when you were the Only Twin. If Sam was here being all useless and pathetic, she'd be fine. But without him she was just a person. A girl. All by herself.

If in doubt, be like Sam. That's what Mum Gen said.

What would Sam do?

'Um,' she said, turning to Nell and keeping her head held high even though she could feel an awkward flush spreading over her neck. 'Could you – would you – help me?'

Nell wavered, glancing over at Nishat and Honey.

Sammie could feel eyes on her cheek; could sense

a soft flutter of giggles behind a doll's hand on the other side of the room.

'Please?'

Nishat looked at Honey.

Honey gave her an amused frown, then shrugged. 'OK. So long as you don't put your fingers up my nose.'

Twenty minutes later Sammie joined the rest of Class Six in the foyer, still in her jeans and T-shirt but now with sticky eyelashes, sticky lips, and a squirt of Honey's cakey smell.

She felt like an alien – but no one else looked like themselves either.

'Very nice, Class Six,' said Mrs McMin, eyeing them all with undisguised horror. 'Miss Townie will enjoy the photographs, no doubt.'

The five-minute walk to the Treetops auditorium through lashing wind and pelting rain, along a skiddy path made of mud, was met with wails of horror – mainly from the boys, who were all swished and preened too, and universally ponged of camel.

The auditorium had been rearranged since the movie night, chairs stacked against the walls, music thumping loud enough to fight the rumbles of thunder outside. There was a spinny disco ball sending loops of light across the floor, and a projector casting swirly shapes on the wall.

Sammie didn't recognize any of the songs.

The boys all stood on one side of the room and the girls on the other – automatically, as if someone had told them to even though no one had.

Mrs McMin danced with Mr Vine, holding hands like on *Strictly*.

It was awful.

Sammie had done what she was expected to. She'd Been Like Sam. But as the dance floor slowly filled up – it felt like falling.

She might as well be in an attic. Or a hole in the ground.

There was a table at the back of the hall, laid with crisps and fizzy drinks and miniature sausage rolls. Sammie picked up a paper bowl of hula hoops and sat underneath the table, eating, watching, bored out of her mind and wishing her eyelashes weren't so flipping sticky.

She texted Sam.

> Have you been murderized by the bad man?

She could leave. She could go home and rescue him. She'd be good at that.

But Sam was apparently quite unmurdered.

> Not yet

Paolo, Alfie and Halid took over the dance floor, re-enacting their Leavers' Assembly breakdancing spinny thing.

Some song came on that everyone knew a dance to: complicated handclaps and bum wiggling.

Sammie put hula hoops on her fingers, and ate them one by one.

More dancing.

More songs.

Then a slow one.

Emily and Reema stood whispering in the corner, giggling.

And then suddenly Emily was dancing side by side with Paolo, swishing her hair and giggling.

Reema was framed against the swirly projector, watching, stricken.

Sammie recognized the look on her face: Kensal Rise Kites versus Finchley Goldfinches, 12–13 at full time, last summer, the moment Reema's corner kick bounced off Sammie's header, veered towards the goal, and hooked just left of the upright.

Disappointment.

Let down.

Failure.

Reema flung her hands up over her face, and fled to the loos.

Sammie ate the last three hula hoops. Then she slid out from under the table, left the thumpy noise and flashing lights of the auditorium, and followed her, the music still pulsing quietly through the door.

She pushed each cubicle door open, one by one.

Inside the third, Reema was sitting on the lid of the toilet, eyes wet, nose red. 'Go away,' she sniffled.

Sammie shook her head. 'Nope. I've come to be your friend again, now Emily's busy. Yay!'

'I don't want to be your friend.'

'Yeah you do. I'm nice now. My mum's putting it in her book and everything.'

Reema sniffled again. 'You were always nice.'

Sammie felt her chest tighten with happiness. But Reema was frowning as she clutched a tissue.

'I just . . . Look, I'm not nine any more, Sammie. I don't like the same things I did when we started being friends.'

'Neither do I.'

That was in the book too.

At the age of nine, Sam A declared an ambition to become the youngest ever striker for Manchester United – but she was going to be a javelinist now. Maturity, right there, on paper. A tadpole grown into a frog.

But Reema shook her head. 'You do, though. You still like running around getting all sweaty. You like stupid jokes and playing games.'

'I could like other things! Like, um . . . boys. And hair. I could pretend.'

'I don't want a friend who's pretending.'

'But—'

It's not up to you, thought Sammie fiercely, her hands forming fists. *I'm going to friend at you anyway. I'm going to friend at you till you crumble and give in and friend right back.*

But now Reema was blowing her nose, blinking the last of her tears away. 'I want a friend who finds me crying in the toilets and asks me *why*.'

Sammie stared as Reema stood up and splashed

her cheeks with cold water from the sink. Then she gave Sammie a worried look in the mirror.

'You won't tell anyone I was crying, will you?'

Sammie shook her head. Reema smiled crookedly. 'Thanks, Sammie.' She pulled her hair out of its ponytail, fluffing it up in the mirror and swishing it around her shoulders. Then she smiled again, properly this time, and pulled open the door, the music booming louder.

'Say hi to Sam, when you get home. And your mums. Give Surprise a kiss on the nose from me. I'll miss him.'

I'll miss you, she meant, really, maybe. *Goodbye*, she meant.

The music faded away as the door fell closed behind her.

Sammie stared at her own face in the mirror: freckles, chin-scar, floppy brown hair tucked behind her ears. Pink stuff on her lips. Black smudges around her eyes. A tadpole into a frog – except apparently after the frog you had to become a teenage girl.

Just when you got the hang of being you, you were supposed to be something else.

It was all a bit exhausting, really.

Sammie splashed her face as well – she wasn't sure why, it just seemed like a thing a teenage girl might do – and patted it with a tissue.

'Right, then,' she said to the face in the mirror. 'Let's—'

The low thump of music outside the toilets stopped with a jolt. The fluorescent light above her head flicked off. Sammie was plunged into total darkness.

Out in the auditorium, someone began to scream.

26

Sam trained the camera on the Bad House, focusing tight in on the top right window as trees waved in the rain.

Rohan peered out. 'You seriously thought I was locked up in there?'

'Reasonable mistake,' said Sam blithely. 'I saw eyes; saw your dad; thought it must be you. Have you ever been inside?'

Rohan shook his head. 'Dad says it isn't safe. The stairs are all falling apart. Why would anyone want to be in a house that's all rotten and horrible?'

'Exactly! That's why it's such a perfect place for a kidnapper to hide his victims.'

'My dad is not a kidnapper!'

Sam sighed, and looked through the camera lens again.

To be fair, it was hard to go on thinking of Mr Grover as the Bad Man when he spent half an hour sitting in his taxi with his head on the steering wheel and his shoulders shaking up and down as if there was a small personal earthquake inside.

It was even harder when a woman in clicky high heels and a suit came running down the street, long black hair flapping behind her. She knocked frantically on the silver car window. Mr Grover got out and they wrapped up in a long hug, with more earthquaking.

'Your mum?'

Rohan nodded, his shoulders shrinking inwards.

'Sorry. I wasn't sure you had one. Because, you know, not everyone does. Your dad always brings you here.'

'Sometimes my mum doesn't get home till late, so she can't. She's an accountant. That's why we moved, for her new job. Dad mostly does picking up and cooking and taking me to stuff. You know, the mum things.'

'My mums say there aren't *mum things*. Just the Person Who Looks After You things.'

'I suppose. He does them, anyway.'

Rohan's mum let out a long sort of wailing sound, and Mr Grover made her sit in the car.

Rohan nibbled his fingernail. 'I suppose my mum does some of the mum things too.'

As the trees lining the street swayed and rustled in the swirling wind, Sam started to feel slightly less Samazing. As the evening grew darker and black clouds rolled in, he could hear Mr Grover out on the street, yelling Rohan's name, in a voice all hoarse and stretched out. Sam remembered walking up the same street, yelling for Surprise when he was missing. He knew what that felt like; the hollow guilty ache inside.

'Are you totally sure you want to be a secret person in an attic?' he whispered.

But Rohan's mouth folded in on itself at the very idea of going home.

Sam heard car doors slamming, and when he peered out, the silver car was driving away.

It was only until Friday.

Sam's phone buzzed with a new text from Sammie.

Have you been murderized by the bad man?

There were three knocks on the attic wall.

Rohan squeaked, and dived under the picnic rug.

Sam pressed his finger to his lips, then knocked back three times.

'Good luck gathering evidence!' came a whisper across the roof, before Pea's window clicked shut.

Rohan's head reappeared from under the blanket, eyeing Sam with suspicion. 'Just how many people know you're up here?'

'I've got a few sidekicks,' Sam said casually, positioning the camera carefully under the window. 'It's what happens if you're someone like me.'

Rohan's eyes flicked around the room, noting the painted spaceship view-screen and the pile of hand-drawn comics. For an instant Sam thought he might be about to say something rude. But instead

he stared at Sam with an eager, rapt expression.

'Sam – what do we do now?'

'Now we wait.'

Rohan crawled across the painty floor to sit next to Sam and stare out. 'Sam, what do you do if you need the toilet?'

'Do you need the toilet?'

'No.'

'Then we'll worry about it later.'

The steady thrum of rain beat down, broken every now and then by a stronger shower that flung itself angrily out of the sky, drumming hard on the tiles over their heads.

Rohan looked up nervously. 'Is this going to be someone's bedroom?'

'I don't know.'

'Will it be your bedroom?'

'I don't know.'

'If it isn't your bedroom, who's going to sleep in it, Sam?'

Sam looked at the cardboard cot in the attic of the doll's house, and hesitated. If he said it out loud, it would be real; a new baby, not just a pine cone. He wasn't quite ready yet.

'Sidekicks are meant to be quiet, Rohan.'

Rohan looked wounded. Then he raised his finger to his lips, grinning behind it. *Shhh.*

Sam grinned back, raising his finger too.

Rohan's hand shot out to grab his wrist.

Sam's gaze flicked to the window at once.

Eyes.

Not just one set of eyes, either. The orange curtain pressed against the glass slid back, and Sam found himself staring into three – no, four – maybe *five* pairs of eyes, all glowing in the acid yellow light of the streetlamps.

'But they can't be . . .' whispered Rohan. 'So many . . . Who are they?'

'I don't know,' Sam whispered back. 'But I think they want us to see them.'

He raised the camera, held it steady, then clicked. *Flash.*

At once the eyes vanished, and the curtain dropped back over the window.

They waited and waited, but the eyes didn't come back. It was as if he'd scared them away for ever.

He had proof, captured on the camera screen: a row of glowing eyes.

Rohan stared at it, bewildered. 'I swear my dad's just a taxi-driving nurse! I'd have noticed if he'd gone all . . . kidnappy.'

'So why are those secret people in your house?'

Rohan licked his lips. 'Maybe they're hiding from something else horrible, like we are. What do we do, Sam?'

What would Captain Samazing do?

Sam took a deep breath. 'I rescued you. We need to rescue them too.'

The wind had begun to snap twigs off the trees, send-ing them skittering and swirling down the street. A distant car alarm went off, then another. The squally rain started up again, longer each time, so hard that it came in through the tilted window and soaked Sam's sleeping bag.  The sky was roiling with fast-moving clouds.

'It's good,' said Sam boldly. 'Noise'll give me cover. There won't be many people around.'

At last he heard the front door slam, then a

hammering on the Llewellyns' front door. Soon after, Mum Gen, Mum K and Pea's mum all set off down the street clutching books and bottles of wine, laughing as the wind whooshed through their hair.

Book club, once a month. They wouldn't be back for hours. It was perfect.

Time to prepare.

Extra bedding. Bottles of water. All the cow biscuits Sam could find.

He pulled on his most Samazing clothes: black joggers, a stretchy black top, his red gloves and his spider-web hat. He pulled on Mum Gen's fuzzy blue jumper too, for warmth, and because it smelled nice.

'Ready?' asked Rohan.

Sam grabbed his torch.

Something was missing. He tried imagining a cape swirling around his shoulders, billowing heroically – but it didn't work.

The picnic blanket. It would have to do. He grabbed it and knotted the itchy ends around his neck.

'OK, Rohan. You need to stay here and keep

watch. Here's the mobile phone. If I don't come back, phone Pea – her number's in there and she lives next door, she'll know what to do.'

'Aye, aye, Captain,' said Rohan, and gave him a little salute.

Sam clanked down the ladder, then slid it back up and pushed the trapdoor back into place with the pole, just in case his mums came home early. He flew down the stairs, the blanket cape billowing satisfyingly behind him.

Surprise bounced up at once, barking joyfully.

Sam longed to stay with him – or to bring him too – but he held firm. 'Stay here, boy. Go on – sit.'

With a whimper, the puppy let himself be pushed away, and moped on the bottom step, head drooping, ears flat, as Sam crept through the front door and pushed it closed with a click.

He crouched on the doorstep, huddled in the blanket against the fierce wind whipping through his hair.

Then he darted across the road in the darkness.

He dropped back under cover behind the bushes in front of the Bad House. It loomed up, the scaffolding creaking and groaning as the rain began again in earnest. Staying close to the crumbly brick wall, he edged closer.

Then a hand reached out from the gloom behind him, and gripped his shoulder tightly.

27

The Treetops auditorium was in chaos.

Sammie stumbled out of the toilets, using the mobile phone as a torch – but she could already hear screams of panic.

'It's the storm, miss!'

'Miss, miss, the power's gone off!'

'What do we do, miss?'

'Ow! You're stepping on me!'

The light flicked across a jumble of limbs and wild eyes as Sammie searched through the crowd. Someone was going to get hurt; Luanna-Bella was crying, people were pushing and shoving, and above it all there was an ominous roaring from outside as the wind lashed the trees and hurled rain from the sky.

Then she spotted what she needed.

A chair, and a bowl of tortilla chips.

Dragging the chair into an empty space, she climbed onto it, pressed the volume button on the mobile to maximum and hit PLAY. Then she emptied the tortilla chips onto the floor and dropped the phone into the bowl, holding it out.

The *Tiny Robot Unicorn Friends* theme song began tooting out of the mobile's tinny but surprisingly powerful speakers – amplified by the bowl.

'*We're robots and we're tiny . . . we're very, very shiny . . .*'

The seething crowd stilled, all faces turning towards the music.

'Oi!' Sammie yelled, flicking the sound off and tilting the screen under her chin, like a lamp in the middle of the floor. 'Shut up, you lot! It's just a power cut. Everybody, sit down. On the floor. Right where you are.'

There was a ripple of dissent, but gradually she heard shuffly noises.

'Good. Now, you've all got phones, so we don't need to be in the dark. Whack 'em on.'

Lights began to flick on around the auditorium:

faces emerged, lit up in a bluish glow. The tension gave way to giggles.

Sammie flashed the phone around, then hopped off the chair to find Mrs McMin, who was lurking palely in the corner.

'Sammie!' she said, placing a rather awkward and trembling hand on her shoulder. 'Good . . . good girl. Now – we'd better get everyone back to the dormitories, I think, while there's still—'

There was a bang from a dark corner, and Lovely Cameron appeared, his froggy hat dripping wet and his T-shirt sticking to his skin.

'No chance,' he said breathlessly. 'There's a tree come down out there – branches flying around everywhere. Power cables must be down: the whole site's gone dark. Not safe. The kids need to stay here, Angie. Probably all night.'

It took Sammie a minute to register that *Angie* was Mrs McMin; she didn't seem like the kind of person who needed to bother with an actual human name. Mrs McMin started to mutter teacherish things, about *inadequate emergency provision* and *unacceptable lack of foresight* – but now that she was called Angie, Sammie could see the quiver of her upper lip, and the nervy dart behind her spectacles, and for an instant Mrs McMin was Mum Gen calling an ambulance, Mum Gen waiting outside the head teacher's office for the third time in a week, Mum Gen waving goodbye on the doorstep clutching a tissue.

'Don't worry, miss,' she said, waggling the lit screen to distract her. 'We'll manage.'

And she climbed back onto the chair and yelled, 'SLEEPOVER!'

The crowd of bluish faces cheered.

Sammie ordered Nell to make a list of everyone, to be sure no one was lost in the rain.

She sent Christopher, Alfie and Halid round to gather up all the coats they could find, to be sleeping bags or pillows.

Nishat collected the food, to ensure that it was fairly distributed.

Cameron unlocked a door at the back of the auditorium, which revealed a gas stove, many cups, and six large tubs of powdered hot chocolate.

'You know,' said Mrs McMin, accepting a cup as Paolo, Alfie and Halid launched into their dance routine for the third time. 'Contrary to popular belief, Sammie, you're actually rather useful to have around.'

Sammie grinned. It was good to be nice (she was nice, it was true, Reema had said so) but perhaps being a loud, brave, handy-in-a-crisis person might be good too.

If there was a small part of Sammie that wished Mum K was there, watching, writing notes, there was another part that didn't mind. Sam A – bold, assertive, prone to standing on chairs and yelling – was already in the book.

28

Sam froze. The hand on his shoulder gripped tighter.

He sucked in a deep breath and whirled round superheroically (with a bit of falling over) to confront . . .

'Pea?'

She was crouched low in a purple raincoat, her curly red hair whipping across her pale face.

'What are you doing here?'

'Same as you, I think,' she whispered back, looking up at the Bad House. 'Did you hear? An eight-year-old boy's gone missing. His dad came and knocked on our door. He looked really upset. And the police came round earlier to check in our shed. Can you imagine?'

Sam didn't want to. The police?

'Then I wondered . . . the eyes that you saw – do you think it's him, hiding up there? Or trapped, maybe?'

'Erm,' said Sam.

There was an almighty gust of wind, and a long, high-pitched wail came from inside the creaking old house.

'That wasn't wind whistling through the scaffolding,' whispered Pea, 'was it?'

There was another sound – like crying gone wrong – up high this time.

'Nope,' said Sam. 'Come on.'

They crept along to the front door. Sam gave it a shove with his shoulder, but it wouldn't budge.

He stared at the ladder leading up to the first level of planks: the first of three, padlocked in place, zigzagging up the face of the Bad House.

'You are a helium balloon, tugging on your string?' suggested Pea hopefully.

Sam gripped the chill metal upright.

Above, there was a long low rumble of thunder.

'I am a helium balloon,' he said.

I am a feather on the breeze.

I am a mackerel, swimming down the stream.

I am Captain Samazing, doing heroic rescue-type stuff, and I am not scared of ladders at all.

He made it up the first seven rungs, with Pea holding the ladder steady at the base, before the nerves kicked in.

'It's just like the ladder up to the attic,' called Pea helpfully. 'You can do that one.'

'The one in the attic doesn't come with thunderstorms,' Sam shouted back, his words whipped away from his lips.

He drove on, and up, and made it up to the first level of flat planks across the scaffolding. He lay down on them, panting. Then he undid the knot around his neck, and bundled the picnic blanket in a heap.

'More aerodynamic,' he shouted.

'Very sensible,' said Pea, following him up.

She was wrong. Sam B was sensible; Sam Boring, Sam Blah. He was bold and brave and utterly Sam A – but it was too windy to explain.

Another series of pathetic, desperate cries drifted down from above, spurring him up the next ladder before he even had time to be a feather or a leaf.

The third ladder was wooden, only seven rungs, widely spaced.

Now they really were up high. The scaffolding creaked. Trees groaned. The planks underfoot juddered, growing slippery as the rain intensified and the sky thundered again. There was a crack of lightning. Sam pressed himself up against the wall of the house, wet palms flat as if they might glue him on, then edged past the first window.

Pea appeared by his side, taking lots of very short quick breaths as raindrops pattered on her raincoat and rolled off the end of her nose. They were up at streetlight level now, and Sam could see two pink spots on her freckly face, standing out against all the pale sweaty panic.

'I'm scared,' she whispered.

'Try Attentive Breathing,' puffed Sam.

Pea joined in, her face pinched with concentration.

They both edged further along the wall, past another tiny window, all the way to the last one.

The curtain hung flat against the cracked glass: faded orange fabric, with black mouldy stuff cling-ing to the bottom. There were speckles of mould on the wooden window frame too, like fur. It must be horrible inside, Sam thought, and wished he still had the blanket. Rescued people always got wrapped in a blanket.

The wind suddenly dropped, and there was a skittery sound coming from within; not the wailing of before, but movement, like tiny frightened footsteps.

Sam swallowed hard, then tapped lightly on the window.

The movement became frantic, like a whole roomful of secret children were cowering away. The curtain pressed against the glass, as if desperate hands were trying to reach out to them. Sam jerked backwards, and had to grab Pea to stop himself from falling down and down. He flung himself forward again, gripping the window frame.

'It's OK! We're here to rescue you,' he whispered. 'I'm opening the window now. Don't be scared.'

With a glance at Pea, he pushed it up. It was the old-fashioned wooden sash sort that slid upwards. There had once probably been a lock on it, but it had rotted away years ago. The window resisted, then gave way and slid up with a thunk.

Pea produced her torch and clicked it on.

The wind picked up again, howling around their ears, and blew the curtain in. Sam grabbed it and swept it aside.

Eyes.

A roomful of eyes, all glowing in the beam of the torch.

Eyes, on a roomful of *cats.*

They were everywhere – every colour, every size: darting across the floor, leaping up an old empty bookshelf in the corner, hopping onto the window-sill to sniff the night air. A nest of kittens was heaped in one corner, fighting and pawing to get close to a big mother cat. The others mewled and moaned and shrieked.

'Cats,' whispered Sam, rearing back from the smell of rotting floorboards and cat-wee as Pea jerked the torch around. 'Just cats.'

Pea grabbed his arm as the scaffolding gave a lurch, the planks under their feet rattling in the wind that lashed cold rain against their legs. There was another vast crash of thunder, then, an instant later, a blinding flash of lightning . . . then an almighty *CRACK!*

Sam turned – just in time to see, across the road, Surprise's favourite weeing-on tree splintering in two. One half remained standing. The other began to fall, with an ominous groan, directly towards the roof of the house opposite.

Sam's house.

Pea clutched his arm ever tighter as she pointed across the gap between the houses.

'Sam – who is—'

Sam just had time to see Rohan's frightened face pressed up against the tiny sloping window of his attic before the splintered tree crashed into the chimney stack, and sent it toppling straight through the roof.

29

'Sam? *Sam!*'

Pea's face was suddenly in front of him, so close he could see the point where each eyelash came out of her skin. She was shouting something, tugging on his elbows, but the storm whirled the words away. All Sam could do was pull back and stare across the space between the houses.

At the jagged-edged black hole where the attic roof used to be.

It was half hidden by the fallen tree; wet leaves and branches sprouted out of the tiles as if it had grown up through the house. But beyond that he could see broken tiles . . . broken bricks . . . the shattered window frame, the glass smashed through . . .

'Rohan? Rohan!' he yelled across the chasm.

The wind took his words too, as the rain slashed down, thunder pummelling the sky again.

He had been at the window. He had been right under . . .

Sam saw a glimpse of light; a tiny blue glow.

The mobile phone. Rohan must've turned it on.

'Come on,' he breathed, crawling across the slippery planks towards the ladder.

'But, Sam,' said Pea, dropping onto her knees next to him, her face streaky with rain and tears. 'The little boy . . . I don't . . . How is . . . ?'

'Later,' Sam panted, shivering as he edged backwards, his foot hunting helplessly for the top rung as he felt the whole scaffold sway. 'I'll explain later. Come on!'

He was a hot-air balloon ride.

He was a shooting star passing close to the sun.

He was terrified.

The rungs were slippery and the wind kept changing direction, buffeting him around and making the ladders judder as he climbed down – first one, then the second, then the third. As he hit the cracked concrete and turned round, the raspberry-red front door of the Llewellyn house flew open, casting a golden glow across the puddles forming in the crazy paving.

Tinkerbell raced out in her mac and rain hat, looking up at the sky with a curious mixture of pride and horror – closely followed by Clover clutching an umbrella, which flipped inside out at once.

'Pea, what are you doing out here?' Clover yelled across the road, fighting hopelessly with the umbrella. 'It's freezing! Wait . . . Sam?'

Sam shook his head and ran past her, legs shaking, his feet tripping over each other now that he was on the ground.

There was a scream, high-pitched, from Tinkerbell. Clover spun, following her gaze, and saw the fallen tree and the grim black hole in the roof.

'Go inside, call 999,' cried Pea through the wind, giving Clover a push. 'Fire brigade – someone's trapped. Tink, go in! And keep Wuffly inside!'

Sam kept running, dodging whirling leaves and scattered branches. The standing half of the old cracked tree stood out, a startling white dagger pointing upwards. The other half had fallen across the front wall and lay sloping like a terrible bridge up to the attic.

He stared desperately up through the rain, yelling Rohan's name.

He tried climbing the sloping half-tree, but it creaked and groaned when he climbed on, and sent the upper branches rattling through the roof, scattering chunks of tile up into the air and hurling them back down to smash on the pavement.

'Bad plan,' he whispered, clambering back down. 'Rubbish plan.'

He stumbled backwards into the road, searching the black hole in the roof frantically for another glimpse of blue light, a sign . . .

'There!' yelled Pea, pointing up.

Rohan's head appeared, then his narrow shoulders – so high, so dangerously high. His hair was white with dust, his eyes so huge with panic they seemed to take up his whole face – but he was there, alive, awake, moving –

Crying.

'It's OK!' Sam yelled as loud as he could. 'Stay there! We're coming! Help's on the way!'

Sam darted towards his front door – but a shower of rooftiles smashed onto the path.

Above, Rohan was edging closer to the drop,

clutching one arm awkwardly as he knelt down beneath the jagged cover of the roof tiles.

Pea's hands flew to her mouth. 'Oh my God. He's trying to climb down.'

'Stay still!' cried Sam – but it did no good. Rohan was grabbing one of the spindly branches. He hooked one thin leg over the edge where the guttering used to be, sending more broken tiles clattering to the ground.

Ladders.

Grabbing Pea's sleeve, Sam ran back across to the Bad House.

But they were all padlocked up, chained into place.

It's not fair, thought Sam dimly. They had ladders. He needed a ladder, and they had three, and he'd even learned how to climb up a ladder, as if he might need to urgently at a moment just like this. Far off he could hear sirens, but they were so faint, so far away, and Rohan was trapped up there, and he wasn't going to die in assembly, he was going to die there in Sam's house, not just in a feelingsish sort of way, but really and truly and for ever, and his dad's shoulders would shake in that earthquake way again, and his mum's too, and . . .

Sam took a breath.

He knew just what to do.

'I am a powerful iceberg on an air current!' he yelled suddenly, and leaped up the first rung of the first ladder. 'I am calm like an eagle!'

He scrambled up onto the scaffolding planks and scooped up the picnic blanket.

'Tell Clover to get pillows! And cushions! Anything soft!' he yelled down to Pea. 'He can jump! We'll hold the blanket over them and catch him!'

He hurried down the ladder and raced over to his front garden, peering up as the rain hammered down into his eyes.

Rohan stared down at him from high up above, still clinging to the spindly branch with one arm, shuffling his feet as if trying to work out the best way down.

Sam tried yelling every version of *stop* he could, but Rohan couldn't hear, or if he could, he was too panicky to listen. Instead, Sam raised one finger to his lips, and held it there, still.

High above, Rohan stopped moving. He raised his finger to his lips too. *Shhh.*

The wind rattled the roof tiles as thunder

shuddered the air, and another crack of lightning lit up the roiling clouds – but they stood quiet for a moment in the heart of the storm.

Then Pea, Clover and Tinkerbell came running out, clutching red sofa cushions and duvets and more blankets. They flung them down in a pile, then Sam unfolded the picnic blanket, and they stretched it out between them like a tartan trampoline.

'What's he doing?' hissed Tinkerbell. 'What's he waiting for?'

Sam shook his head. He knew how high up it felt, looking out of the attic. Rohan was scared. Anyone would be scared.

'You are a snowflake, slowly drifting down,' he called up.

You are a seagull on an air current.

You are a leaf on the breeze.

Rohan jumped.

30

SECRET #11:

Sam woke up in Pea's front room in borrowed pyjamas, his head resting on two warm hairy dogs.

Pea and Tinkerbell were there too, curled at either end of the sofa, fast asleep.

He brushed doggy hairs off his head with a 'Ptheh', and sat up.

His arms hurt.

He felt shivery.

His tartan blanket-cape lay abandoned in a corner.

The image of Rohan flying down towards him played back in his mind – along with the agonized yelp he'd let out when he hit the blanket. Then the blue flashing lights had arrived – at the same moment as three bewildered mums came running down the street, and his mums discovered that their home contained one less roof and one more Sam than they'd expected.

He wasn't sure which one they were crosser about.

Sam would've liked to phone Sammie, to consult on how best to be in this much trouble – but then the door creaked open, and Pea's mum peeked in.

'Oh good, you're up. Come and have breakfast, my chick. I think your mums would like a little chat.'

They were gathered around the kitchen table, Mum K still in last night's rumpled jeans and MS MARVEL T-shirt, Mum Gen in someone's dressing gown, both looking oddly smeared by exhaustion, as if he'd done them in 6B pencil and wiped his thumb across the paper.

He hoped it might be a hugging sort of conversation.

It was not.

'I don't even know where to start,' said Mum Gen weakly.

'Sorry,' said Sam.

'Oh well, everything's all right then, so long as you're sorry,' said Mum K, her voice cold.

'Kara,' said Mum Gen gently.

'What? Don't be angry? How can I not be angry? The scale of deception . . . lies . . . Seeing that poor little lad going off in an ambulance . . . You could've been killed! Both of you!'

'Very sorry,' said Sam quietly.

'I mean, I expect this of your sister. But not you. Not our lovely sensible Sam.'

'I'm not sensible!'

'Evidently!'

Mum Gen put her hand on Mum K's. 'Quite. But the recriminations can wait. I want to know why.' She laid her other hand on Sam's. 'How did we get here, Sam? Why ever would you lie to us like that?'

So Sam explained, quite slowly, about the DEATH SLIDE OF DOOM – and about Attentive Breathing, and being a soap bubble, and how he actually could not, at all, have gone to Treetops with Mrs McMin.

'So I hid. Then Rohan came and hid too, so I said he could stay. I didn't know the police would be looking for him. And I definitely didn't expect a tree to fall through the roof.'

'Well, no, I don't think any of us saw that one coming,' said Mum K.

'Thank heaven you weren't both up there,' said Mum Gen with a shudder. 'Why *were* you out on that scaffolding?'

Sam told her about the eyes, and the secret, hiding, potentially kidnapped people who were cats after all.

It did sound sort of crackers, now he was saying it out loud in Pea's kitchen.

Mum Gen looked pale, her hair wispier than ever. 'Behind every front door lies a secret,' she said eventually. 'Sometimes ones even the people living inside don't know about, hmm?'

Sam shrugged one shoulder unhappily. 'I know I shouldn't have kept all those secrets. Sorry. Really sorry. But – I actually was a bit heroic, in between lying and being the Bad Sam. I was actually Samazing. Not like boring Sam B in your book. Not like a sidekick at all. You should put that in, Mum K, so people know.'

Mum K and Mum Gen exchanged looks.

'Oh, *Sam*,' said Mum K.

After that, it apparently *was* a hugging sort of conversation.

The doorbell rang, accompanied by a rattling of the Llewellyns' letterbox.

Wuffly and Surprise scampered down the hall, barking madly until Pea and Tinkerbell hurried out in their pyjamas and held them back so Pea's mum could answer it.

It was Mr Grover.

'The firefighters next door told me this was the place to knock?'

Rohan appeared from behind his broad back, peering out anxiously.

Pea's mum shooed them inside at once. 'Of course. Come through – tea? Breakfast?'

Sam shuffled up to make room round the kitchen table as the house filled with toast smells and the clatter of mugs.

Mr Grover sat opposite, his flashing grin replaced by the same smeared look as the mums, with a scruffy beard beginning to grow on his chin. Rohan tucked in beside Sam. He had a plasticky blue cast on one arm, held in a cloth sling, and a few papery stitches on a purple bump on his forehead.

'Broken arm, couple of bruises, bit of a scrape here and there. Got lucky, didn't we, Ro?'

Rohan dipped his head, looking as if he might like to climb under the table.

Mum Gen murmured a few words very quietly, and everyone looked politely away so Rohan wouldn't feel stared at.

'Does it hurt?' whispered Sam into Rohan's ear.

He hesitated, but the rest of the table had started a conversation about the relative disgustingness of hospital food. He leaned in close, his breath tickling Sam's ear as he whispered, 'It did when they moved my arm for the cast. But not now.'

'I'm sorry. Like, really sorry.'

Rohan grinned. 'No worries, Captain.'

Mr Grover cleared his throat. 'Rohan has something he'd like to say, don't you, mate?'

Rohan licked his lips, suddenly anxious again.

He leaned in and whispered into Sam's ear.

Sam nodded. 'Rohan says he's very sorry he was a secret person in our attic.'

Mum Gen smiled. 'Thank you, dear. We're very sorry for almost crushing you to death with a falling chimney. Which is a sentence I never want to say again.'

'Sam . . . I think you might have something you'd like to say too?' said Mum K meaningfully.

Mr Grover looked at Sam, his single glossy curl

falling over his forehead as he leaned in and rested his bulgy arms on the table.

'Um,' said Sam. 'Sorry for thinking you were a Terrible Kidnapper. Though . . . why *did* you sneak into your house in the middle of the night?'

'Sam!' said Mum Gen.

Mr Grover smirked, then glanced at Rohan and looked vaguely guilty. 'You remember that house Rohan drew the first time he came here?'

'With the cat?' Sam nodded. 'Ohhh. Was that Rohan's pet? Were you trying to catch him a new one?'

Mr Grover laughed. 'Nah, mate. Socks was *my* cat. I love 'em. Always had a cat, ever since I was a kid: Mittens, Cookie, Mr McFlufferson.' He stroked his arm dreamily, as if imagining a big furry cat there. 'But – well, we had to leave poor old Socks behind in Melbourne when we moved here. The builders told me there was a bunch of strays living in the house; the missus wanted me to call in

someone to get 'em all put down. But I couldn't bear it. So – I've been nipping in every now and then, between taxi jobs. Putting down some food, trying to get 'em to use a litter tray, sneaking a few kitty cuddles. They're nippy little beggars, no lie.' He waggled his fingers, showing thin red scratches on them. 'Once the builders need to get inside, I'll have to pack them off to a shelter, I guess. Unless we can talk your mum into keeping one or two – right, Ro?'

'Are you *really* going to live in the Bad House?' asked Tinkerbell, reaching for the last piece of toast.

Rohan looked at Sam, then whispered.

'He doesn't like it when you call it the Bad House.'

'Sorry,' said Pea. 'We'll definitely stop. Are you going to go to Sam and Tink's school when you move in?'

Rohan looked sweaty at the very mention of *school*.

'No, it's OK,' Sam said quickly. 'Our school sounds way nicer than yours. Well, Miss Townie is. She's my teacher. She'd never make you do assembly if you really couldn't.'

It felt odd, talking for Rohan when he knew he could speak – but he understood. With every new ladder he still needed to be a lily pad or an eagle in his head. Even after going up the scaffolding across the road, he wasn't sure he could do it again. For Rohan, it must feel like that every time he started a new sentence. It wasn't something you could just fix and forget about.

Tinkerbell rolled her eyes. 'Mrs McMin would. She's *awful*, Rohan. Once she drew a spot on the wall and made my friend Angelo put his nose against it for a whole hour, just for talking. And she keeps a snotty hanky in her pocket and wipes the whiteboard with her germs. And Jade Johnson's sister says that at PE they were trampolining and a girl broke her ankle and Mrs McMin made her keep on trampolining until her foot actually fell right off her leg.'

'That's nothing!' came a loud voice, banging through the front door. 'I've seen her in her nightie and it is the scariest thing *ever*!'

'Sammie?' called Mum Gen. 'What – you're back?'

Sammie appeared in the doorway, dragging her suitcase.

'Treetops fell down in the storm. Well, bits of it did – sorry, Mum Gen, I had to leave your Christmas cardigan behind because it had broken glass on it – so we had to come home early. Only no one answered the phone, so Mrs McMin dropped me off. Now. Sam – why are you eating biscuits with the Bad Man? What have you done to my house? And now there's a big hole in the roof, where's the baby going to sleep?'

31

Dear Sam,

I sort of missed you.

From Sammie

'What baby?' said Mum K.

'*Your* baby,' said Sammie, flinging her suitcase down on the floor. 'And don't bother lying, because me and Sam worked it all out ages ago – even though we totally should've been consulted first if there are going to be babies all over the place.'

'Wait – who's having a baby?' asked Pea's mum, picking up Surprise.

'Er – we are, allegedly,' said Mum Gen, looking alarmed.

'Congratulations!' said Mr Grover.

'No we're not,' said Mum K, waving away Mr Grover's offered hand with a baffled smile. 'I'm not—'

Sammie rolled her eyes. 'Oh, so it's *you* this time, is it?' she said, staring accusingly at Mum Gen. 'That makes it even worse! It won't even properly be my sister. Or brother, if you're having a boy one.' She wrinkled her nose disdainfully.

'No one is having a baby!' shouted Mum K.

Surprise gave a little whimper and bolted out of Pea's mum's arms to hide behind Tinkerbell's knees.

Sammie glared at both mums. 'Where's it gone, then?'

'Nowhere!' said Mum Gen hotly. 'Why ever would you think there was going to be a new baby?'

'Because of the new bedroom in the attic! And the box from the hospital, with the new rabbit toy, and you being all secretive and sneaky and lying to our faces. Obviously. Duh.'

The kitchen fell quiet. The smirky smiles vanished from Mum Gen and Mum K's faces. Mr Grover coughed politely and said he ought to get Rohan back home for a rest. Pea's mum ushered Pea and Tinkerbell upstairs to get dressed, and to wake up Clover.

Surprise jumped onto at Mum K's lap, licking her face, but she didn't shoo him away. She looked down and stroked his ears.

Mum Gen reached over to stroke them too.

'I think it's time,' said Mum K quietly.

'For what?' demanded Sammie.

Mum Gen went on stroking the puppy's head, scruffling his ears. Then she set her shoulders and looked up. 'For you to know the truth,' she said stiffly. 'Come on. We've got something to show you.'

Sammie didn't want to step into her own house.

Treetops had been creepy enough in the morning: broken bits of tree strewn around, shattered windows of their old dorms. It was hard to fathom now. The storm had passed and the sky was back to a sunny blue – but here too the evidence was everywhere: a pile of soggy cushions in the front garden; branches and leaves scattered across the pavement; the jagged half-tree still standing like a spear in the street. The branches that had plunged through the roof had been sawn into pieces and piled into the skip over the road, leaving a gaping black hole opening the attic to the world.

Sammie could just make out strange, dusty paintings on the attic wall, surrounded by chimney rubble. 'Wow, Sam,' she said, looking up. 'That looks way scarier than anything we did at Treetops.'

Sam looked vaguely sick.

After Mum K had checked that it was safe for them to go inside, they trooped in, Sammie lifting Surprise safely into her arms.

The attic ladder was down, and the landing was once again filled with rained-on boxes and rubbish rescued from the debris: Sam's sleeping bag, now grey with brick dust; the old doll's house; a sticky plate.

'Gosh, you kept busy,' said Mum Gen, gingerly climbing the first few rungs of the ladder to peer in.

'I was going to paint over all the stuff on the walls,' said Sam as Mum K knelt down to open the doll's house. 'Honest.'

'Why are my legs made of cheese?' Mum K held up the Lego firefighter.

'I was just filling time,' said Sam quickly when Sammie found the pine cone in its attic bed. 'Not playing. Not really.'

'You were imagining a possible family: quite understandable,' said Mum Gen softly, picking up the snow-white rabbit with the gentlest touch, and dusting it off. 'And as it happens, not so far removed from the truth. Sit down, you two.'

Sam and Sammie sat down on the landing, Surprise resting his head on Sam's knee. Mum K tugged the *HOSPITAL* box out of the pile and knelt down next to Mum Gen. She reached out to squeeze her hand, just once.

'Do you remember asking why you're both called Sam?'

'Duh. Only about a million times.'

'You said it was because you couldn't find two names you both liked,' said Sam. 'On that list.'

Mum K flipped the lid of the box and pulled out the handwritten list of baby names. 'It's just an old piece of paper,' said Sammie, scrunching up her nose as Mum K placed the list on the floor and delved into the box again.

'No it's not,' said Mum Gen, smiling as Mum K

picked up a familiar old photo: Mum Gen with short brown hair, her arms wrapped around Mum K's huge baby bump, both beaming. 'It's memories. Sad ones, but ones we wouldn't want to be without. You see – when we wrote that list, we didn't need to think of two names we both liked. We only needed one.'

She pulled out another picture. This time it was Mum Gen with the bump, and Mum K gleefully hugging it.

Sammie found herself holding onto Surprise very tightly, feeling glad of the fast little heartbeat inside that warm, hairy body.

'I had to go into hospital a bit earlier than expected,' said Mum Gen. 'They knew something wasn't quite right. And when the baby was born, it wasn't breathing properly, and they had to take it to intensive care.'

Sammie nodded slowly. 'Like those fish-tank things?'

'That's right. And the baby had to stay in the fish tank – they're called incubators – to get help with breathing, and be given special lung medicine. It was frightening. We called that baby Sam, because it was our best and favourite name. And then, after eleven days, Sam died.'

A little gasp came out of Sammie, without her knowing it was there.

Mum K reached for her hand and gave her little finger a squeeze.

Mum Gen managed a small smile. 'After a long wait, and lots of thinking, we decided to try to have another baby. And we ended up with two! Two beautiful children to love and look after, who needed names – and we still didn't like any of the ones on our list as much as Sam. So we decided you could be Sams too. And then the baby would always be with us, in our thoughts, every day.'

Sam made a sniffly noise. 'That's too sad,' he whispered.

'It is, yes,' said Mum Gen. 'That's why we never told you; because it makes us sad to think about it. But we always planned to tell you, one day. It just got harder, the longer we left it.'

'Even mums have secrets sometimes,' said Mum K, ruefully adjusting her glasses. 'Now, do you have any questions?'

'Was it a boy or a girl?' asked Sammie.

'Does it matter?' said Mum K with a smile.

'Um. Only a bit,' said Sammie, chewing her lip in case mattering even a bit wasn't allowed.

But Mum Gen smiled. 'The other Sam was a little boy.'

'Oh,' said Sammie, her shoulders drooping. Then they drooped even lower. 'It didn't matter. I'm still sad.'

'Was that his, then?' asked Sam, pointing at the snow-white rabbit tucked beside the pine cone. 'The other Sam's?'

Mum K nodded, touching the tips of its ears with the lightest brush of her fingertips. 'Yes. I bought it the day . . . He couldn't have toys like this in the incubator, because of germs, but . . . we thought he might be well enough to come home, so . . . It's a present he never got to have.'

Mum Gen reached into the *HOSPITAL* box and brought out another smaller box, with a tiny hat, a pair of mittens and a white onesie with a yellow duck sewn onto it. 'He wore this, though.' She let them both touch it.

It was so small, Sammie thought. Too small to imagine. She tried holding her arms cupped together to hold a baby so small, and it seemed impossible. Her baby brother. Her big brother.

'You should put him in your book,' she said firmly. 'Right at the beginning, so everyone knows.'

'Quite right too,' said Mum K, with a sniff. 'In fact – I need start the whole thing over. I should be writing a book about two dopey mums who keep secrets from their children, ignore the things they're really worried about, and don't even notice when there's a secret twin hiding under their noses – despite the suspiciously large amount of cheese disappearing from the fridge.'

'Yep,' said Mum Gen ruefully. 'In fact, for a pair of child psychologists, we seem to be wholly inadequate at looking after our own.'

'Does that mean *we* can be in charge instead?' said Sammie.

'No!' said both mums together.

Sammie sulked for a moment. 'OK. I suppose I did sort of miss you a bit while I was at Treetops. Mrs McMin does rubbish tucking in.' She yawned. 'And she kept calling me *Sam*. Although . . .' Sammie thought for a moment. 'Actually I don't want to be Sammie any more. I want to go back to being Sam, now I know why I was one. Is that OK?'

'Fine by us!' said Mum K, beaming.

'Now then,' said Mum Gen. 'After all that, I think we're entitled to second breakfast.'

They all scrambled up.

'Hang on,' said Sam. 'If there never was going to be a new baby . . . what is the attic for?'

Mum K grinned. 'For all of us, you daft pair!'

'But we've *got* bedrooms,' said Sam.

Mum Gen nodded. 'Yes, and that's fine for sleeping. But I know what a pain it is for you all having the consulting room at the front of the house, especially now that I'm working longer hours. You always have to keep quiet; Kara needs the study now she's working here in the week too. And it's an awful squash fitting the four of us onto those bean-bags at the end of the kitchen. So we wanted to have a comfortable family room. Somewhere we can all relax together – watch *Tiny Robot Unicorn Friends* . . . drop popcorn all over the floor . . . make a mess no one can complain about . . .'

Mum K rolled her eyes, then threw up her hands in defeat.

'A family space, that's what it's for. And we

thought it would be a fun surprise – no, I don't mean you, you dopey dog – so we kept it a secret. Which now seems a rather unwise move. What do you think, Sammie? I mean, Sam?'

'Well. OK. But I think it needs a new roof.'

'Agreed. Sam?'

Sam hesitated. 'Will there be proper stairs as well? Or always a ladder?'

Mum Gen smiled. 'Which would you prefer?'

One Sam looked at the other.

'Ladder,' said Sam.

'Stairs,' said Sam at the exact same moment, laughing.

That was the thing about being twins. You were the same, but different, always.

TWO WEEKS
LATER . . .

'How was it, how was it?' called Mum Gen, already hopping on the doorstep as they walked home from their very last day at Orchid Lane Primary.

'Well . . . ' said Sam.

Luanna-Bella had spent morning break colouring in her hair with green and purple marker pens, and then fainted due to fumes and had to be carried to the nurse's room.

Halid had sellotaped his leg to a chair, to see if it made his foot go numb. (It did.)

Paolo lent all the boys his new deodorant spray – *Oriental Spices*, it said on the can, though Sam thought it smelled like the back of a cupboard – and Christopher ran around flapping his armpits at Honey all afternoon. (She was unimpressed.)

And it was all topped off by the Class Six Leavers'

Assembly: an explosion of tubas, singing, and an interpretive dance entitled *The Great Treetops Storm* that left even Mum K discreetly weeping in the audience.

'We gave Miss Townie flowers and a card,' said Sam.

'I drew it,' said Sam.

'She cried,' said Sam.

'Not because of my drawing, though,' said Sam quickly. 'Just because she's sad and will miss us.'

Mum Gen wailed, her hands to her mouth. 'I can't believe I couldn't be there!'

Mum K smiled, and waved her mobile phone. 'I recorded the whole thing. Wasn't going to let you miss out on the fearsome McMin demonstrating an actual human emotion.'

Mrs McMin had cried too.

'Eh, she's not so scary,' said Sam, flicking her hair. 'I mean, obviously she's still a *bit* evil. But it's hard to be scared of someone once you've seen them hanging upside down off an abseiling wall like a big screamy bat.'

Sam sighed. He would've liked to see that. In fact, there was quite a lot of Treetops he'd have liked to try – the famous bacon; duck-stroking; meeting Lovely Cameron, whose face was now plastered all over Sam's bedroom wall in grinning photos – especially knowing that no one else had ended up going on the DEATH SLIDE OF DOOM after all.

Also, he could not look a cow biscuit in the face again.

It had been, as Mum Gen had declared, a learning experience for all of them.

Mum K unhooked Surprise's lead, and he scampered gleefully up the stairs.

'Oi, no fair, you weren't supposed to start without us!' said Sam, stomping her feet as she followed him up. 'And I wanted blue walls!'

The hole in the roof had been fixed, and on the landing, instead of a silver ladder and a trapdoor, there was now a new extra staircase, narrow but quite secure-feeling, leading straight up. Inside, the attic was taking shape as a real new room. There were rollers and brushes everywhere, and the clean fresh smell of new paint.

'Don't get stroppy, madam; the white paint is just for the stairs,' said Mum Gen as they all climbed up.

Mum K unrolled a new set of plans, with furniture ideas sketched onto them. 'Now. I'm thinking a low sofa there . . . Maybe a TV on the chimney breast?'

Surprise had curled up in a patch of sunlight under the new, wider sloping window.

Sam gave him a stroke, then tipped open the window to look out.

The Bad House was a distant memory now. The roof across the road was complete too: there were brand-new windows in place, and although it wasn't ready to move into yet, it already looked like any ordinary part of the street. Not Bad. Just a house.

Rohan was sitting on the front step, a ginger cat curled up on his lap.

Sam gave him a wave.

He grinned, and lifted the cat's paw to wave back.

'I told you. Blue!'

'Why this insistence on blue?'

'Because it's my favourite colour!'

'Sam, not everyone wants to have a room painted in someone else's favourite colour.'

'Well, you should, because it's the best, and anyone who thinks stupid purple or yellow or whatever is better than blue is a stupid poophead.'

'*Sa-am.*'

'Ugh. *Fine.* I'm sorry for calling you a stupid poophead. This was wrong because—'

'Sam, you're the artistic one: what do you think?' Mum Gen held up two pots, one deep violet, one a bold, bright yellow.

'Neither!' said Mum K. 'Listen, a soft green . . . like Minty the robot unicorn . . .'

Sam flung her hands over her ears.

'Well . . .' said Sam slowly, looking around the room. 'There are four walls. And four of us. Why don't we paint one each?'

Sam dropped her hands, perking up at once. 'With whatever we like?'

He could have his *Pocket Rocket* spaceship viewscreen back; the farm; all of Class Six at Treetops.

Mum K raised an eyebrow at Mum Gen.

She shrugged. 'Why not? One each.'

'And the ceiling for Sam,' murmured Sam, looking up.

It would have stars, he decided. And clouds, and feathers, and soap bubbles, all lightly floating up.

MUMS' BOOK

INTRODUCTION

This book is by us. It is about two mums and their Sams.

Mum Gen is pretty, even though she has bits of grey hair, good at talking to unhappy people (and even people who don't talk at all), and quite smiley. She is kind but a bit messy.

Mum K is good at plum crumble, quizzes, and dancing in the kitchen like an idiot. She is a bit mean (only a bit) but quite funny as well.

They are both learning to be more honest and truthful and not to keep secrets. We are hopeful that as they get older, we can teach them never to put hummus in our sandwiches.

HELLO READERS,

I hope you enjoyed reading Sam and Sam's adventures. You might like to know that before they had a whole book to themselves, the Paget-Skidelskys popped up in four other stories, all about Pea, Tinkerbell, Clover, their not-at-all cheese-like Mum – and Wuffly the dog, of course.

Turn the page for a little taste.

Happy reading!

Susie xx

PEA'S BOOK
of Best
FRIENDS

CHAPTER 1

GOODBYE

'There,' said Pea, propping up her creation on the mantelpiece. 'Told you I'd have time to finish it.'

She stepped back and considered her handiwork. It was a blue plaque – the sort they put outside houses where famous writers once lived, to make people say 'Oh!' and fall off the pavement. This one was more of a blue plate, really. The writing was in silver marker that was running out. She'd spelled *Author* wrong due to the pressure of the moment – but it would do till there was a real one.

'It's *nice*,' said Clover doubtfully, peering over

the top of Pea's head. 'But why isn't my name on it?'

'Mine isn't either,' said Pea. 'Or Tinkerbell's, though I suppose I could add us. Somewhere.'

'Don't bother with mine,' said Tinkerbell, clicking one end of a pair of handcuffs closed around her tiny wrist. '*I'm* not going anywhere.'

With a click, the other cuff snapped shut around the fat wooden leg of the sofa.

With a gulp, the key disappeared down Wuffly the dog.

It was the day the Llewellyn sisters were to leave the sleepy seaside town of Tenby for their new life in London. So far, it was not going exactly as planned. The electricity had been cut off a day too soon. Tinkerbell's father Clem (who had stayed overnight just to keep an eye on things, as he often did lately) had made a bonfire in the front yard to cook toast over, stuck on the end of a twig, and accidentally set fire to the front door. The removal van had arrived three hours early, and left without warning, taking with it breakfast, their hairbrushes, and all but one of Clover's shoes.

But not, apparently, a pair of handcuffs.

Pea was secretly pleased. Clem had put out the fire before she could dial 999, but now they had an excuse. Perhaps she could locate a kitten for the firefighters to rescue too, while they were in the area. In gratitude, they might offer to take them by fire engine all the way to London, sirens on. That would be the ideal introduction to city life.

City life was something of a mystery to Pea, but she couldn't wait to meet it. She'd made everyone play Monopoly after tea for weeks, for research. London seemed to be mostly about rent and tax, going to jail, and being a top hat. Old Kent Road was brown. According to films, there were also red buses, Victorian pickpockets, and all houses had a view of Big Ben. It was going to be brilliant.

Have you read all the Pea Books?